Mary Neville

Arthur, or, a knight of our own day

Vol. 1

Mary Neville

Arthur, or, a knight of our own day
Vol. 1

ISBN/EAN: 9783337291990

Printed in Europe, USA, Canada, Australia, Japan

Cover: Foto ©Andreas Hilbeck / pixelio.de

More available books at **www.hansebooks.com**

ARTHUR

OR,

A KNIGHT OF OUR OWN DAY.

BY THE

AUTHOR OF "ALICE GODOLPHIN."

"Indeed he seems to me
Scarce other than my own ideal knight."—TENNYSON.

IN TWO VOLUMES.

VOL. I.

LONDON:
CHAPMAN & HALL, 193, PICCADILLY.
1876.

ARTHUR;

OR,

A KNIGHT OF OUR OWN DAY.

CHAPTER I.

'I have no men to govern in this wood,
That makes my only woe."

TENNYSON.

A PRETTY little Rectory, nestling under the shadow of the South Downs. There are hundreds like it in England, almost too well known to need any particular description. Who cannot picture to himself the long, low, brick house, the colour of the brick picturesquely varied with weather-stains and lichen, and for the most part nearly covered with creepers? The broad, velvety lawn in front, with two or three gay flower-beds, and its one grand horse-chestnut rearing its leafy head--the pride of the Rectory garden. Facing all this— so near that it seems less than its real distance (nearly half a mile) from the house— rises the broad, swelling, green down. "Flocks of quiet sheep are feeding" here and there, and occasionally, by dint of close watching, you may discern the form of the shepherd moving about with his shaggy dog at his heels. Over all spreads the clear blue sky, flecked with small, fleecy clouds, gradually assuming a rosy tinge towards the west—for it is now evening, and the day is far spent. Pretty, soft white clouds—how well they have done their appointed tasks all day!—sometimes sailing kindly between the earth and the too scorching rays of the sun; sometimes distilling in refreshing drops of rain to moisten the thirsty ground, and now, all their work done, they are hastening to the west to array themselves in their gorgeous evening robes of scarlet and gold—part of that glorious pageant displayed every evening before our unobservant eyes—the setting of the sun !

> " To Fancy's eye it seems to prove
> They mantle round the sun for love."

Some such thoughts as these are passing through the mind of old Mr. Helmore, the rector of this little village of Arling, as he sits in his trellised porch, enjoying the soft evening air, which comes to him laden with the sweets of heliotrope and mignonette. A book is lying on his knee, but he has closed it now, and slipped in a rose-leaf as a marker. It has long been too dark to read—too dark, at least, for him ; for in spite of his vigorous, upright form, and clear, steady blue eye, he is a very old man. Several years more than those allotted by the Psalmist as the limit of human existence have passed over his venerable snowy head, yet is his " eye not dim, nor his natural force abated." Any moderately skilled physiognomist would tell his character at a glance. The square, well-deve-

loped brow shows thought, sagacity, and
much benevolence ; and the somewhat large
mouth, with its well-cut lips and remarkably sweet smile, combined with the mild
but searching glance of his eye, proclaim
him a kind man, but not one liable to im-
posture, or likely to be easily deceived.

His features and expression are accurately reproduced in his eldest daughter
Elizabeth, who has lighted a little taper,
and is now working away busily at the
round table in the Rectory drawing-room.
By the huge pair of scissors in her hand,
and the pile of violet-spotted and striped
cottons on the table at her side, it is evident that her occupation is one eminently
suited to her father's daughter. She is
cutting out frocks and pinafores for the
poor people. How deftly the delicate
fingers fly about their work ! and with
what a bright, happy glance she looks up
occasionally to address a remark to her
younger sister at the further end of the
room.

Elizabeth Helmore is now three and

twenty, but this younger sister cannot be more than eighteen. She is half lying, half reclining, on the sofa near the window, her golden head thrown far back in the endeavour to catch the last rays of light upon her book, which is that most fascinating of old-fashioned novels, Miss Burney's "Evelina." The Rectory library does not produce many story-books, but, such as they are, they are eagerly read and conned over by this young lady.

How lovely she is! Let us take a quiet survey of her beauty as she lies there, in utter unconsciousness of being observed.

Elsewhere you may have met with a complexion as fair and transparent, features as regular, hair as brightly golden and wavy; but where, in broad England, will you find a smile such as Ida Helmore's? —like a living sunbeam; or that half-loving, half-defying glance of her dark-blue eyes, which finds its way at once to your heart, and takes you straightway captive by sheer force of its sunny sweetness! Even in her present unstudied attitude, which would

have been awkward in any one else, you
can see that her form matches her face in
its perfect grace and beauty, badly set off
as it is by the plain holland gown, which
she has contrived, nevertheless, shall fit
closely and neatly enough on the rounded
outlines of her waist and shoulders.

Elizabeth's clear voice now sounds across
the room, breaking the profound silence
which has been reigning hitherto.

"Do shut your book, or come to the
table, dear Ida. It is so bad for your eyes
to strain them over that small print by this
light."

"You dear old fidget, I will come in a
minute."

"I wish you *would* come and help me
with these frocks; they ought all to be
ready to-night. Come, Ida, you have had
enough of ' Evelina' for one day."

No answer, she is deep in her book again.

Elizabeth waits a few minutes, and then
speaks with a little impatience—only a
little—for the sweet composure of her face
is quite unruffled.

"Ida, do come to the light, you will read yourself blind."

Ida pays absolutely no attention, but at this moment Mr. Helmore enters the room, and his quiet mandate causes her to lay down the book without delay.

"I have some news for you, girls," says the old clergyman, standing with his back to the fireplace, in the familiar attitude of an English gentleman, though no fire burns now in the polished grate: "the Atherstones arrived at the Grange last night."

"How many of them?" inquires Ida, eagerly.

"Only Sir Henry, and his son, Captain Atherstone. Miss Atherstone is obliged to remain at Torquay."

"Oh! then they will not be here long?"

"I should say not; but I have heard nothing about their plans. Elizabeth, my child, how industrious you are; you have been cutting out those frocks all day."

"Oh! she likes doing it," said Ida impatiently. "Father, dear"—and she went up close to him, and laid her hands coax-

ingly on his arm—"tell us a little more.
What is Captain Atherstone like? Is
he handsome — as handsome as his father?"

"How can I tell, Ida? He has been in
India with his regiment for seven years;
and a young man alters so much at his age
in a foreign climate."

"I dare say he is yellow, and lean, and
shrivelled up" (in a disappointed tone).

"Possibly. We shall be sure to see them
in church to-morrow. Elizabeth, will you
light the candles in the study?—I have
much writing to do to-night."

Elizabeth rose, and, having arranged
everything for her father's comfort in his
own room, and seen him established in the
huge, old-fashioned writing-chair, she returned to the drawing-room, to find Ida
again stretched on the sofa, a look of discontent on her fair face.

"One never can get anything out of
papa," she began. "What do *you* say,
Elizabeth? Are our new neighbours likely
to be any sort of acquisition to us?"

"I should not think we are likely to see much of them. If Miss Atherstone had come——"

"Miss Atherstone—she is only an invalid."

"Yes; we might have been of some use and comfort to *her*."

"That is just like you, Elizabeth. I do not believe you would ever care to know anybody, if you did not think you might be of some use to them."

"Or they to me," returned Elizabeth, with a quiet smile.

"Now, I feel differently;" and Ida rose, and, throwing the sash window widely open, stood gazing out on the deepening twilight. "You may look amazed, Elizabeth, but I say it is only natural for us girls, mewed up as we are in this dead-alive place, to welcome the advent of any stranger, more especially if he is a young man, rich, well-connected, and good-looking,"

"He may be perfectly hideous, for all you know about it."

"Nonsense! how could an Atherstone

fail to be good-looking ? Oh, Elizabeth !
see ! come here-—quick !"

Elizabeth rose in some alarm, and hastened to her sister's side.

The Grange gardens almost bordered on
the Rectory grounds ; and just underneath
the wall, barely within sight, a dull red
light was seen passing slowly to and fro.

" He is smoking," exclaimed Ida : " that
is the light of his cigar. He *must* be nice,
Elizabeth—nice men *always* smoke !"

"You goose !" smiled her sister ; "you
quite frightened me. I thought the pigs
had got into the garden again. Do come
to the table, Ida, and don't waste the evening in watching the light of a cigar, especially as it is just as likely to belong to the
steward, or to old Sir Henry, as to Captain
Atherstone."

Somewhat crestfallen, Ida turns away
from the open window, and, sitting down
at the round table, endeavours to follow
her sister's advice—that is to say, she again
opens " Evelina," and actually reads nearly
three pages. Then she lays down the

book, and looks up with wistful, troubled eyes.

"Elizabeth, do you suppose that any two girls of our age (of course I mean *ladies*) ever led such dull lives as we do?"

"I should think many have done so," replies Elizabeth, in a low, half-pained voice. "You have said that so often, lately, Ida; and, after all, I cannot see that you have anything to complain of. We have many kind neighbours—I do not mean merely people who accidentally live close to us, but real *friends*; and as for gaieties, our summers are always cheerful: we have been quite dissipated this June."

"Five croquet parties and three dinners," replied Ida, in a dolorous tone. "And what sort of people do we meet when we do go out? Widowers and old married rectors abound; but it is a fact that we do not reckon one presentable young man among our acquaintance. I do not count the young Palmers, who are always living on the verge of bankruptcy, or Mr. Sanders, with his red hair and freckled visage, but I can state positively that this part of Sussex does not produce one single eligible, *marriageable* young man."

"Are you so *very* anxious to be married, dear?" asks Elizabeth, looking at her with a wistful light in her grey eyes.

"Elizabeth, you are the only person in the world to whom I could say such a thing; but I declare solemnly to you that I pray, actually *pray*, every night that I may soon be married; or if not that, that something else may happen to take me away from this place. I am sick of these downs and fields, sick of this house, sick even of the horse-chestnut on the lawn. I am sick of seeing you eternally bending over your work, in the same holland gown and the same blue bow; I am tired of seeing father doing the same things every day in just the same manner. Oh, dear! I know it is all very ungrateful and horrid, but I weary of *everything*; I feel sometimes as if the air of Arling were choking me."

Elizabeth does not answer at once: she

cannot, indeed, for her heart is very full, and she has much trouble to suppress the hurt, indignant tears. After a minute or so, however, she looks up with a bright, kind smile.

" It *is* dull for you, dear, very dull. We will try and manage some change for you this year; I think it can be——"

But the sentence is never finished, for Ida sees the signs of grief in the kind eyes that have so seldom looked· reproachfully upon her, and, springing up, she throws her arms round her sister's neck, and exclaims, in a smothered, repentant tone—

" No, no, Elizabeth, dear, you shall arrange nothing. I shall get on very well here, indeed. I was only—only *joking.*"

But Elizabeth knows better; and though she only smiles and smoothes the golden hair back from her sister's fair forehead, she silently begins an abstruse and lengthy calculation of ways and means. Her sister shall not mope if she can help it; if any amount of pinching and paring in that already frugal household can afford her the pleasure of a few weeks' change, it shall be done, and done soon.

Elizabeth and Ida Helmore had no mother. She had died about five years before this story begins, bequeathing her own romantic name and brilliant beauty to her younger daughter—the only legacies that were in her power to bestow. Mrs. Helmore's most indulgent acquaintance (strictly speaking she had no *friends*) could not pretend to say that her death was really a misfortune to her daughters. Ill-tempered, ill-educated, owning no law but that of inclination, no constraining power but that of impulse, it was a standing wonder that the sensible, clear-judging Mr. Helmore should have selected such a woman for his wife. ˙ Well, he had married very young, and at that time Ida Davenport was a bright, taking girl, with fascinating manners, and a beauty which might well have turned a wiser head than that of the young curate of five-and-twenty. So they were married, and the amount of happiness produced by their union may be best conceived from the fact that for nearly ten years Mr. Helmore daily thanked Heaven that he had no children to be contaminated by the daily intercourse and companionship of his wife.

Then two sons were born, but they died before either came of age ; and then, after another long interval, Elizabeth and Ida were sent to cheer the desolate parsonage-house. Mrs. Helmore had little to do with their training : her health was failing rapidly, and their education was confided to nurses and governesses, always carefully selected by their father.

Poor man ! it was his constant endeavour to keep the knowledge of their mother's character from his children, and to a certain extent he succeeded. Always patient, always forgiving as he was, ever ready to welcome his wife back into his large, tender heart, if she would but have given him a little love and confidence in return, it must still have been a great, though unspoken, relief when at last Death relieved him of an almost life-long sorrow, and Ida Helmore, once so beautiful and so tenderly beloved, was laid to rest in Arling churchyard.

Mr. Helmore's case is, unhappily, not a singular one. It is astonishing how very few really good mothers there are in the world. Tender fathers, kind brothers, loving unselfish sisters, are often to be met with, but where is the ideal mother to be found? The kind, wise, tender soul, to whom every one in the house looks for counsel and guidance—whose very presence is cheering and invigorating like a sunbeam—to whom her daughters—aye, and her *sons*—turn naturally for sympathy and advice—and to whose clear judgment her husband may safely trust his household and his affairs.

Are many such numbered among your acquaintance, my reader? No; nor in mine. There are scores of fond, weakly indulgent mothers, selfish mothers, worldly mothers, *nervous* mothers, who make their nerves an excuse for avoiding every duty, human and divine, and giving way to ill temper and acerbity on all occasions. But in the higher ranks of society—I speak exclusively of them—good mothers are rare indeed.

Let English matrons look well to the high and honoured name they bear—let them try to be in all things what they would have their daughters to be—let them throw away the shackles which pride, or fashion, or imaginary ill health, may have thrown round them—and so act that, in the last Great Day, they may give in a good account of the fair jewels committed to their care !

What a long moralizing digression ! With it let this chapter end.

CHAPTER II.

"So we grew together
Like to a double cherry, seeming parted."
Midsummer Night's Dream.

SUNDAY morning—one of the brightest
and sunniest of all that bright sunny
August, but intensely hot. Even inside
the shady little village church the heat has
managed to penetrate, and the atmosphere
feels exhausted and sleep-inspiring even
before the service begins.

This is partly owing, no doubt, to the
unusually large congregation. All the village have assembled to see "t' old Squire,"
for the news of his arrival has been duly
circulated among his loyal tenants; and as
he very seldom visits Arling, not a man,

woman, or child would willingly be absent on the occasion of his advent.

This is a conservative little village, and the old-fashioned reverence and affection for the hereditary landowner, now unhappily dying out in many parts of the country, exists here in all its ancient intensity.

Punctually at five minutes before eleven the bells cease, and the harmonium peals forth a voluntary, softly and soothingly played as all voluntaries should be, calculated to calm the minds of the congregation, and attune their thoughts to the solemn service about to commence.

A young lady sits at the instrument which is placed in the chancel, tolerably well sheltered from observation. By the dark, neat braids of her hair, and the graceful sweep of her low shoulders, as well as by the pale, good-looking profile that is occasionally visible, you may recognize Elizabeth Helmore.

Ida sits by herself in the Rectory pew, and just now she is earnestly trying to preserve a duly stiff and decorous attitude, but her eyes often wander to the door with a look of eager expectation. She is watching, watching intently : no village maiden in all the congregation is more inquisitive, more full of eager curiosity than she.

The voluntary is just ended, and Mr. Helmore, looking quite patriarchal with his white robes and snowy, stately head, has just moved forward from the vestry to the reading-desk, when Sir Henry Atherstone arrives, and walks slowly up the aisle, leaning on his son's arm. They enter the Grange pew, and Ida raises her eyes, and takes a hasty but scrutinizing survey of the new comers. She sees a tall, noble-looking old man, evidently of a great age, but upright as a dart ; indeed, so upright and firmly does he stand, that it seems as if he must have leant on his son's arm more as a token of affection than because he felt the need of any such support. A grand-looking old man, an almost perfect specimen of the " fine old English gentleman " —a race now, alas ! well nigh extinct.

But surely he will have a not unworthy successor in his eldest son. Captain Atherstone's features may not be as strictly regular as his father's, but he has a broad, open brow, and there is something peculiarly fascinating in the glance of his fearless blue eye.

By the end of the first lesson Ida has discovered that he has bright brown wavy hair, and an upright stalwart figure, not quite as tall as his father, but withal taller than the generality of men. Even Elizabeth has not been able to resist an occasional glance at the Grange pew, and what she notices there has pleased her as much as Ida, though they have not been observing quite the same things. She might not have been able to tell you accurately the colour of his eyes and hair, but she has seen with pleasure that the young heir of Arling joins devoutly in the service, and finds the places for his father in the prayer-book and hymn-book—time-honoured articles, with huge print and mouldy purple

binding, which have lain unused for nearly
five years.

His friends are sorry to see that the old
Squire's sight is fast failing him, and he
looks altogether sad and preoccupied. Even
during Mr. Helmore's brief, energetic sermon his eyes wander away, and are often
fixed on a marble tablet let into the wall
opposite the Grange pew. His old eyes
cannot see so far, but all Arling knows the
inscription on that stone :—

"Near this place lie the remains of George Henry
Atherstone, eldest son of Sir Henry Atherstone, of this
parish, who died May 5th, 1860, aged 20.

"Also of Alfred Mordaunt Atherstone, who died June
1st, 1861, aged 20.

"Also of Blanche and Emma Catherine Atherstone,
who both died December 25th, 1870, aged 19."

Yes, four of the Squire's own children lie
there. It seems almost as if some evil destiny hung over the Atherstone family, for
all were born healthy and blooming enough,
and all have faded away with the same
incurable disease—all, that is, but the two
now surviving. One of these is now sitting

by his father, and the other, Mary, is hopelessly ill at Torquay, fast following in the
steps of the others. No wonder the old
Squire looks worn and sad : in a few weeks
he will have but one child left. All the
village knows this, and it causes a certain
tender, almost reverential, sympathy to
mingle in the kindly, respectful glances
they occasionally cast at " t' old Squire."

Through the service Captain Atherstone's
eyes scarcely wander from his book; or if
he raises them at all, it is to look up at
the painted window opposite (erected by
his father in memory of his dead twin sisters), or else to glance into the body of the
church, apparently in the hope of recog-
nizing some old friend of his boyish days.
Never once does he glance at the Rectory
pew, and the fair-haired girl sitting alone
there. Ida observes this, and is mortified,
forgetting that in the deep, old-fashioned
seat she occupies very little of her can be
seen, except a white bonnet and a twist of
golden hair.

After service they meet in the church-

yard, and Sir Henry shakes hands kindly
with Elizabeth, cordially with Ida, glancing
at the younger sister with an expression of
mingled astonishment and admiration. Indeed, Ida is a pretty picture of the ideal
clergyman's daughter this morning, in her
simple thick white dress and black mantle
—neat, inexpensive, and most becoming.
As she stands in the porch, her dark blue
eyes modestly cast down, the sunlight falling in a golden shower on her fair waved
hair, she is as beautiful as a dream—

      " A sight to make an old man young."

"I have not seen you for five years, Miss
Ida," says Sir Henry, smiling. " I scarcely
recognized you at first ; you are so much
grown, and — improved. Arthur, these
young ladies were both old playmates of
yours once, though they seem to have forgotten you. Ah ! there is my good friend
Helmore."

The two old acquaintances greeted each
other cordially, and walked together down

the little narrow path, leaving the young ones to follow behind.

"It is a long time since you have been to Arling, Captain Atherstone," observes Elizabeth, for lack of something better to say. "You must have nearly forgotten the old place."

"Indeed I have not," he replied, warmly, "I have forgotten *nothing*. Every tree and cottage is as familiar to me as it must be to you. I remembered your face, Miss Helmore, though I dare say you did not know me."

"You did not remember *me*?" asked Ida, glancing up at the young man's fair, handsome face.

"Yes" (with a smile). "I have not seen you for nine years, and of course you are more changed than your sister; but I knew you at once. It is just the same face, only older. I could fancy now that the old days had returned when we used to run races together, and got into disgrace for climbing the cherry-tree in the Rectory garden and breaking two of the largest branches."

"Do you remember that ?" said Ida, laughing. "What fun we used to have ! I wish for some reasons that the old days could come back again !"

"So do I," answered the young man, looking down at her beautiful face. "I have never had such fun since."

"Do you stay long at the Grange ?" inquired Elizabeth.

"I fear only a few days. My father has a good deal of business to get through, but I can do most of it for him, so he may very likely leave me here for a short time, and return to Torquay himself. He is anxious to be as short a time as possible away from Mary."

"Is she *very* ill ?"

"She does not grow rapidly worse, but there is no doubt that her strength is steadily declining. My father grudges every hour spent away from her bedside."

Elizabeth looked up, her soft eyes full of sympathizing tears.

"I had no idea she was really dangerously ill ; I am so sorry for you all."

"Thank you; I am sure you are," he answered, simply.

They talked a little more on indifferent topics, and then parted at the Rectory gate. Sir Henry and his son walked together down the lane, and, strange to say, the father was the first to remark—

"That is a lovely girl, Arthur; I never saw any one so much improved. Were you not surprised?"

"She is very pretty," replied Captain Atherstone, briefly.

"*Pretty!* Good gracious, Arthur! one would think you were as old as I am, to hear you talk. I tell you she is the handsomest girl I have seen since I went with your mother to Court in '52."

"Is she?"

"Indeed she is. Arthur, my boy"—and the old man glanced affectionately at the handsome young face beside him — "I should like well to see you married before I die, and to just such a girl as Ida Helmore—fresh, innocent, beautiful, and just eighteen."

The young man smiled.

"If I were immediately compelled to choose one of them as a companion for life, father, I am not sure that I should select your favourite. Miss Helmore would not, I suppose, be considered beautiful, but there is something very nice about her face. And I should never care to marry a beauty."

"Not a stuck-up, spoilt, airified London beauty, perhaps, but a simple country girl like this——. Well, it is rather premature to discuss the subject. How well that plantation is looking, Arthur; it must be thinned this autumn." And the conversation drifted into other topics.

According to the wont of summer days in August, the afternoon is rather hotter than the morning. Evening service is not till seven o'clock, so the Miss Helmores have a good four hours and a half to themselves after luncheon. They have spread a large rug under the shade of the horse-chestnut on the lawn, and are occupying their leisure hours in different characteristic ways. Elizabeth is sitting upright, using the rough, gnarled trunk of the old tree as a back, Her head is bent low over her " Christian Year." She is not content with a superficial reading of one of the most beautiful poems in that lovely but mystical book, but is trying hard to find out its exact hidden meaning. Ida is lying prone on her back, her hands clasped behind her head, which is well set off, in all its golden beauty, by the dark background of the rug. Her eyes are fixed on the sky—not brighter or bluer than themselves. Apparently she is engaged in the profitable occupation of trying to count the little white clouds that are vainly endeavouring to temper the fierceness of the sun's rays. She must have good eyes to be able to gaze so long and so steadily into that dazzling empyrean.

" Have you no book, Ida ?" asks Elizabeth, looking up. "Shall I fetch you something to read ?"

" I *have* a book, thank you," is the low, dreamy answer. " I am trying to read the words that the leaves are writing against the sky."

"My dear child! what nonsense!"

"Nonsense! why? If there are 'books in the running brooks,' and 'sermons in stones,' why may not leaves have a language of their own as well? There, now, I see it distinctly. Just bend your head this way, Elizabeth, and you will see a word written as clear as print. That tiny twig and leaf together makes A, then R, next comes T, then H (don't you see?), U, R.—Can anything be more clear? The leaves are saying 'Arthur.'"

"I cannot see anything of the sort," replied Elizabeth; "you are in one of your romantic moods, Ida, and see signs and tokens in everything. Why should the leaves spell 'Arthur' more than any other name?"

"I know why," answered the girl, slowly raising herself from her recumbent position till she stands erect on the grass; "but I shall not tell you. I think I shall take a turn in the kitchen-garden, Elizabeth; it is not so hot now."

"You will be burnt as brown as a berry,

and get a headache into the bargain. Be advised, Ida, and stay where you are, cool and comfortable."

"I can't stay in one position all the after-noon : it makes me stiff. Perhaps I shall find some peaches on the south wall—they will cool me more than anything. You won't come ? Good-bye, then."

And she strolls away, humming a song, assuredly not to be found either in Tate and Brady, or the "Ancient and Modern Hymn Book."

Elizabeth gazes after the graceful retreat-ing figure till it is lost to sight behind some tall laurustinus, and then returns to her book.

All alone, Ida wanders on, down the shady gravel path, and out into the full glare of the kitchen-garden. How hot it is here—oppressively, almost painfully hot! What a dreamy, humming noise the bees make as they lazily float—not fly—in the heavy, sultry air, occasionally darting their long trunks into some peculiarly tempting rose or honeysuckle, but assuredly doing no

real hard work. Perhaps it is Sunday with
them ; or perhaps—to take a more prosaic
view—the heat has dried up the sweet moist
juices of the flowers, and there is little food
left, even for a bee, in their dry and droop-
ing cups.

Ida begins to think of sunstrokes, and is
on the point of retracing her steps, when
her eye is caught by a yellow, downy ball,
just peeping out from behind a sheltering
leaf on the warm south wall. With an exclamation of delight she springs forward,
and in another moment her white teeth meet
in the cool, delicious flesh of the first peach
of the season. There are others within
reach, but none quite ripe ; and she is pur-
suing her researches along the sunny wall,
when an event occurs which causes her to
stop short and look up in surprise.

The event is a very common one, not
calculated in itself to produce either astonishment or alarm. It is simply a whiff of
tobacco-smoke, wafted over the wall, and
sending a light, odorous cloud full in the
girl's face.

Apparently such an accident has never happened to Ida before, as it appears to her in the light of a very choice joke—at least, one may infer this from her conduct. Throwing away the half-eaten peach, she tosses back her golden head, and bursts into a fit of merry pealing laughter—to an impartial observer perhaps sounding a little *too* loud to be quite natural. It has its effect. A man's voice comes—apparently—from the other side of the wall, speaking in a tone of almost ludicrous dismay.

"Miss Ida, is that you? Have I annoyed you by my horrid smoke? I apologize a thousand times."

"Where in the world are you?" she exclaims, looking up and down and on every side. "Have you put on the invisible cap? or——oh!" as she is suddenly conscious of a whiskered and moustached countenance within two feet of her, and perceives Captain Atherstone cosily half seated, half lying on the top of the wall, his tall form well concealed by the branches of a wide-spreading beech tree that grows on the other side. "How *did* you get up there?" she asks, looking up at him with bright, eager eyes.

"I climbed up by means of a ladder, and have been very comfortable ever since luncheon. You have no idea how nice and warm it is up here."

"Warm! I should think so. How *can* you bear the heat? You will get a sunstroke. You know there *are* such things in England."

"Oh, no; I enjoy it. It is like my native climate. I could almost fancy myself back in India again. To tell you the truth, I was nearly asleep. Pray accept that as an apology for having sent a stream of smoke right into your face."

"Perhaps I may forgive you some time," she laughs. "Come down and eat some peaches."

"Do you mean it? May I really?"

"Haven't I asked you? I am sure you have smoked quite as much as is good for your health. Come down."

She looks so pretty, standing there with

upturned eyes, no unfit personation of our mother Eve, with the downy fruit in her hand, her fair, loosened hair looking more golden than ever, with the sun shining on and through its silken masses.

A sound of scrambling and scuffling, during which two branches of Mr. Helmore's favourite peach-tree are broken short off, a high and almost perilous leap, and he stands before her, hot, panting, and triumphant.

"No joke, that jump," is his first remark, as he wipes his warm brow. "What a height these old walls are !"

Now she has got him she does not quite seem to know what to do with him, but lowers her eyes, and stands in a bashful silence, which is very pretty and becoming, but rather unsatisfactory.

He glances at her half amused.

"Where are these peaches?" he asks, smiling. "I will never forgive you, Miss Ida, if you have brought me down on false pretences."

"It is a very good thing for you that I

3—2

brought you down on *any* pretence," she retorts, the hot carnation in her cheeks gradually fading to a more natural and becoming hue. "It can't be good for you to smoke so many hours; and how can you tell that Sir Henry does not want you, and has not been searching for you high and low ?"

"Oh, no; he has not wanted me. If he had he would have summoned me. Did you notice the little gold whistle that hangs at his watch-chain? When he wants me he sounds that twice, and I can hear it distinctly in any part of the grounds."

"How odd! just as if you were a retriever," says Ida, laughing.

Captain Atherstone has no answer to make, but the tone of her remark does not quite please him. They walk on silently, till the lady speaks again.

"No one would imagine you had been in India, Captain Atherstone: you are not in the least tanned. I expected you would

have come home either copper-coloured or a
dusky yellow."

"Ah! I was brown enough at one time,"
he replied ; "but I had a fever just before
coming home, and it is wonderful how ill-
ness alters the complexion. When I recovered I was as fair—as you are; no, not
quite that," he adds hastily, glancing down
at the delicate pink and white loveliness
beside him.

"Were you very ill ?" she asks, looking
up at him with blue, pitying eyes.

"Very ill, indeed. I should think no
one could be worse who did not die after
all. I am glad I got well after it," he adds,
looking up dreamily into the sunny sky
above them.

"I suppose you are !"—laughing.

"Not entirely for my own sake," he replies gently ; "I was not thinking of myself at all, then : but it would have been a
desolate thing for my father to be left *quite*
childless in his old age."

They stroll on, a little subdued for some
minutes, and then other topics of conversa-

tion arise, and an hour slips pleasantly away. At last Ida glances at her watch, and exclaims in surprise—

"Five o'clock! They will be waiting tea for me, Captain Atherstone; I must *race* home. Good-bye."

Seeing her haste, he makes no attempt to detain her, and she flies away like a lapwing, and enters the Rectory drawing-room just as tea is placed on the table.

"How late you are, dear!" says Elizabeth. "Have you been in that hot garden all this time?"

"Yes; it was not so *very* hot."

"The peaches must have been very enticing."

"So they were; *very* enticing."

Meanwhile Captain Atherstone strolls slowly back to his own grounds, this time choosing the more prosaic but safer mode of entrance by a gate in the lane, instead of a flying leap over the wall.

"That is a pretty little girl," he muses to himself; "but it was a regular ruse about the peaches. Just the sort of thing most girls would have attempted ; but somehow one does not expect Mr. Helmore's daughters to be quite like other girls. I wish I had seen Elizabeth."

CHAPTER III.

" Yourself were first the blameless cause to make
  My nature's prideful sparkle in the blood
  Break into furious flame."

T<small>ENNYSON</small>.

R<small>AIN</small>—heavy, persistent, hopeless rain. Those lovely August days have passed away, and September has commenced his mild but gloomy career, decking the russet woods indeed with "a sunshine of their own;" but their brilliant colours can scarcely be distinguished through the thick fog which dismally envelopes the whole country. The Rectory garden is almost swamped; there is a large pool under the horse-chestnut tree, large enough to float a child's toy-boat; and the flower-beds, a week ago so neat and bright, look now all draggled and soaked, the drenched, soiled leaves falling every moment to the ground.

The drawing-room is all confusion to-day, for the Misses Helmore are taking advantage of the wet morning to get through a little business. Piles of old dresses, jackets, and cloaks are to be seen in every direction, covering the chairs and even the floor. There is a sewing-machine on the table, and on the rug lies a grey merino dress, which Ida is inspecting with an air of extreme gravity and anxiety.

"It is no use, Elizabeth," she says, impatiently at last, contemptuously spurning the despised garment with her foot; "I can never make it look respectable. You *must* get papa to give us new dresses this autumn."

"I know he cannot afford it," replies Elizabeth, quietly, without raising her eyes from her task of unripping the torn and soiled lining of an old black silk skirt. "Indeed, Ida, I think we ought not to ask him; those dresses are not really shabby, except just under the arms and at the back of the sleeves, and if we have them mended neatly and dyed——"

"I am sick to death of all this piecing and dyeing and contriving," exclaims Ida; "surely papa might afford us a couple of guineas apiece to make ourselves look decent —I would not ask him for more. It is so particularly aggravating, just now, too, when I—when *we* want to look our very best."

"Why should we want to look our 'very best' just now?" asks Elizabeth, raising her calm eyes in astonishment. "It is just the dullest and quietest time of all the year."

Ida's cheeks are glowing as she turns away, and replies hastily—

"Oh ! I don't know ; we are seeing more people just now."

"Ida, you are dreaming ; we have not seen a soul for a fortnight, except, of course, Captain Atherstone."

"Well"—and Ida turns round, and answers half shyly, half defiantly—"I should not like *him* to think we dressed shabbily ;

men *do* sometimes notice these things, and it would not be very pleasant if he wrote and told his sister Mary that the Rector's two daughters were got up like farmers' wives."

" Poor Mary Atherstone! she has other things to think of !" sighs Elizabeth ; "and I do not suppose Captain Atherstone will trouble himself as to how we look. He appears to me to be profoundly indifferent to everything except his father and his cigars. Will you come here, Ida ? I want to try on this body. I won't keep you a minute."

Ida complies, and it so chances that she is standing before her sister, a half-made body pinned on her slender shape, her fair hair all tossed and tumbled, when a tap comes gently at the window, and a young man's voice is heard, familiar enough now to both the sisters.

" Will you let me in, Miss Helmore ? I am dripping wet."

With an exclamation of dismay, Ida wrenches herself from her sister's hand, dislodging all the carefully-placed pins, and rushes away through the open door.

Returning in five minutes duly clothed and tidied, she finds Captain Atherstone warming his feet before the fire, comfortably sipping a glass of sherry, which Elizabeth's hospitality has pressed upon him.

" I hope my sister has apologized for the untidiness of the room," says Ida, advancing with that easy grace of manner which is vainly imitated by many in the great world, but seemed to come naturally enough to her. " I assure you we don't always live in such a state of chaos."

" I highly approve of your industry," replies the Captain, laughing. " Miss Helmore tells me you make all your own things, and I know, to my certain knowledge, that you clothe half the village."

" Elizabeth is very fond of parading our imaginary virtues," replies Ida, a little crestfallen. " We *don't* make all our own dresses—at least, I don't."

" Don't you ? Well, it is a very useful

talent; I wish my sister could do it. Miss
Helmore, as you tell me you go in so
strictly for economy, I wonder you begin
fires so early in the year."

"That is the one thing Elizabeth is extravagant about," said Ida, eagerly; "she
will have a fire if it is the least chilly, even
in June."

"Not for myself," says Elizabeth, gently
—"it is for papa. You know"—turning
to the Captain—"his throat is extremely
delicate. He cannot bear damp weather or
cold rooms."

"We know how much to believe of that,"
laughed Ida.

Captain Atherstone glanced at her as
she stood by the fireplace, her head a little
bent, the firelight falling on her golden hair
and fair, perfect features. Her crimson
lips were curled in merry scorn, and there
was a covert sneer in her blue eye—a lovely
picture, but scarcely a satisfactory one.

Elizabeth made no reply to her sister's
remark, but, after a short pause, she said—

"If you are really wet through, Captain

Atherstone, you had better change your things at once. Indeed you have been very imprudent to wait so long. Papa is in his study; shall I ask ?——"

" No, no, thanks; don't trouble yourself; the rain was only a good excuse for stepping in here. You can't think how warm and cosy you looked as I passed the window; so different to our great, dreary, half-furnished room."

" I am sure this is dreary enough," sighed Ida. " Oh, how sick we are of this place !"

" Is Elizabeth sick of it ?" the young man asked, turning to her; and then adding quickly, " Excuse me for saying Elizabeth; it slipped out somehow. You are so little altered, that it seems only the other day since we played together like brothers and sisters. You won't be offended ?"

" Oh, no ;" but the sweet face flushed as she bent closer over her work, and she did not give him the permission he hoped for.

" You have not asked if you may call *me* by my Christian name," said the gay, ring-ing voice on the other side. "Is only Elizabeth to be so honoured?"

He smiled. "I meant to ask you, too. Let the subject be settled now once for all. I will call you both Elizabeth and Ida, and you shall call me Arthur."

"Agreed," cried Ida.

"As you please," said Elizabeth, a little coldly; "we *are* very old friends."

The young man looked disappointed, and, leaving his warm seat, he walked to the table, and began to look at some of Ida's drawings which were lying about.

She soon joined him, and the two entered into an animated discussion; for Captain Atherstone considered himself something of an artist (as most young men do once in their lives), and thought he was qualified by his knowledge of the art to apply gentle criticism and discriminating praise.

After about half an hour so employed, he took his leave, and Ida, at once laying aside her gay manner, came to sit on a stool at her sister's feet, and gazed thought-

fully into the fire.   After a time she said—
"Elizabeth, is it not three weeks since
the Atherstones came ?"

"Just three weeks."

"And during that time, how many visits
has Captain Atherstone paid here ?"

"I really don't know, dear ; I have not
kept count of them."

"Then I will tell you.   Twenty at least ;
very often twice in one day.   Elizabeth, he
must be very much taken with one of us :
which is it ?"

Elizabeth looks up with heightened
colour.

"Don't say those things, Ida ; some people
would think you meant them."

"I do mean them.   It is all very well to
talk about old friends and that sort of
thing ; but do you suppose any young man
would haunt a house like Arthur Atherstone does this, merely because his father
has known ours for about fifty years ?   It
is absurd !"

"I do not see that you have any right
to attribute such motives to Captain Ather-

stone, dear. Candidly, I do not see that he prefers one of us to the other."

" Candidly, Elizabeth, should you not be very glad if he did ? Should you not think it an immense thing, an *immense* thing, for the family if he were to fall in love with one of us ?"

" I don't know."

" Elizabeth, you are too provoking. Come, be rational for once in your life, and say that it would be a good thing—a glorious thing. The heir to a baronetcy and fifteen thousand a year ! Why, papa would——"

" He would say that his little girl was talking great nonsense," said a grave voice. and, turning hastily round, Ida saw her father standing in the doorway. " You are a vain, foolish child, Ida. If you were a few years older I should say more. Let me hear no more such unladylike conversation, or I shall have to be ashamed of my daughter. Elizabeth, I want you for a moment. Come to the study, will you ?"

Elizabeth rose, and Ida went to her

room in high dudgeon. Not caring to go downstairs till positively summoned by the dinner-bell, she drew a chair to the dressing-table, and, taking up a hand-glass, gazed long and earnestly into her own lovely face—no unfrequent or uncongenial occupation with her.

" Surely he will love me !" she murmured half aloud to herself. " I never set my mind on a thing in my life, but I obtained it sooner or later. Let him try to be indifferent and cold, if he can ; his manner to me will alter soon—it is altering even now. Let me but have another week— one short week more—and he will be mine —my own ! Perhaps he loves me now— who can tell ? But if not, he will soon— he must—he *shall !*"

CHAPTER IV.

"As she fled fast thro' sun and shade
The happy winds upon her played,
Blowing the ringlet from the braid ;
She looked so lovely, as she sway'd
The rein with dainty finger tips."
TENNYSON.

NEXT day rose bright and sunny, and after breakfast Ida announced her intention of driving into Daylesford, the town nearest to them, in order to make some purchases necessary to the completion of their autumn wardrobes.

"You had better let John drive Dobbin," said Elizabeth ; " he has not been out for three days, and will be rather fresh."

" Can't you come ?"

"No, dear Ida, it is impossible; I want every second of my time this morning."

"Then I shall go alone. I hate a tête-à-tête with John. I always feel as if I ought to say something to him, and I don't know a bit what to talk about. I have no turn for conversing with the lower orders. Besides, I can drive as well as he can."

" 'Being so very wilful, you must go,' " quoted Elizabeth, with a smile. "I never knew you to alter a decision, Ida, or even resign a whim, to please anybody."

"No, I am one of the 'Positive Club,' whose opinions, once expressed, are as unalterable as those of the Medes and Persians."

And off ran the young lady, and appeared in about half an hour dressed in a tightly-fitting black jacket, admirably suited to display the graceful proportions of her perfect figure, and a black hat, ornamented with a small blue feather. To be sure, the jacket had been bought second-hand two years ago, and the hat, like the Revised

Code, had been altered and improved till it retained very little of its original shape and material. Still, both were yet pretty and becoming, and the fresh young beauty would have been still bewitching with much shabbier surroundings.

"You are rather smart to drive into Daylesford by yourself," observed Elizabeth, glancing at the blue feather.

"Never mind," was the gay reply; "it is always well to be on the safe side, and if one is well dressed, one is never taken at a disadvantage. Who knows if I may not come across 'Mr. Right,' as Eva Fletcher used to say."

Elizabeth smiled, the half-puzzled, half-pained smile with which she usually met Ida's sallies.

" 'Mr. Right' would appreciate you all the more if you had a veil on when you were driving in the town. Do, Ida, dear; that hat is no shade at all to your face."

The girl wilfully shook her head and took her seat in the pony carriage, gathering up the reins in a scientific manner, which showed she was no novice in the art of driving.

"I don't half like your going alone," said Elizabeth again, as she stood in the porch shading her eyes from the sun with one hand, while with the other she patted Dobbin's sleek chestnut neck. "At any rate, the horse ought to have been exercised; look at his ears."

"He always cocks them in that way when I am going to drive him," laughed Ida. "He knows he will have to go at a pretty good pace. Good-bye, dear old woman, take care of yourself." And in another moment they had rounded the corner at a sharp trot, and were speeding along the high road at a pace which scarcely permitted Elizabeth's last words to reach her sister's inattentive ear.

"Be sure, Ida, and avoid the viaduct at half-past one. That horse will not stand the express train to-day."

How delicious it was rushing through the sweet autumn air that lovely morning, the fresh smell of the moist earth pervading the breeze; that subtle, indescribable fragrance which is surely only experienced in an English September day after a night of heavy rain. Ida's spirits rose higher and higher. She was only eighteen; she was very beautiful, she had no trouble on her mind to disturb or harass her, and she was being carried through the air without any exertion to herself at the rate of eight miles an hour. What more is necessary to describe the perfection of earthly happiness? As they neared the town Dobbin relaxed his efforts from a smart canter to a sober trot, by his mistress's desire as much as his own, for she wished to look about her, and make sure of passing no friends by unobserved. It was market day, and the little town, usually almost oppressively clean and tidy, was crowded and dirty enough, the narrow streets almost blocked up with carts, driven cattle, and a few— very few—gentlemen's carriages. Out of the window of one of these a hand was extended as Ida passed, and a lady's voice called—

"Ida Helmore, is that you? Stop one moment; I have a note for your father."

Ida drew her reins tight, so peremptorily checking Dobbin's career, that the little horse resented the interference by straightway rearing almost on end, and shaking his glossy mane in displeasure. Ida was used to his vagaries, and remained perfectly composed, but the lady by whom she had been addressed uttered a scream of terror, and exclaimed—

"Good heavens! what an awful creature! Don't leave him, Ida, I will get out." And in another minute she was standing in the street, a tall woman, dressed entirely in black, with a long, melancholy nose, and small, short-sighted blue eyes, a tolerably ladylike but unprepossessing-looking person.

"Mr. Helmore ought not to allow you to drive that animal, my dear," she said, gingerly shaking hands with Ida; "it is not really safe, and on market-day too!"

"He did not know I was coming."

"Then, Elizabeth——"

"Oh, Elizabeth is a dreadful old fidget! I never attend to what she says. Dobbin is amiable enough, it is only his play. Did you say you had a note, Mrs. Fletcher?"

"Here it is; it is only to ask you all to dinner on Thursday week; and you might have taken a message, but I like to do these things in a respectful way, especially to a clergyman."

There was a patronizing ring in her sharp voice which made Ida toss her proud little head as she replied,

"No one can accuse *you* of informality, Mrs. Fletcher——"

"I hope not, my dear. If cleanliness is next to godliness, I am sure courtesy is next to cleanliness. Are the Atherstones still at Arling?"

"Sir Henry leaves to-morrow; I believe his son will stay a few days longer."

"Oh, indeed! I suppose you see a great deal of the young man? Bless me! here are some oxen. How I do hate this town on a market-day! Man! keep your beasts in

order, can't you see they want to come on
the pavement ?"

"Don't be afraid, Mrs. Fletcher," said
Ida, laughing; "they are quiet enough.
How are you, old fellow ?" and she actually
gave a fat old ox a prod in the side with
her whip handle, thereby causing the
animal to defeat the designs of his driver
by charging down a bye-street.

Amid the shouting and confusion that
ensued Ida managed to get away, and proceeded down the street at a gentle trot,
leaving the hapless Mrs. Fletcher to struggle
against the crowd till she reached her own
conveyance, without having enjoyed the
bit of gossip which had induced her to
leave it.

As she gained the door a dark handsome
head drew back from the window, and a
young man's voice exclaimed,

"Who is that girl ?"

"Ida Helmore; have you never met
them?"

"No, never had the luck; she's marvel-
lously nice looking, whoever she may be."

"They will all dine with us on Thursday week, for the first time this year I am ashamed to say. She *is* a nice-looking girl, but very bad style. Only imagine her driving into Daylesford by herself on a market-day. I call it a forward and un-ladylike proceeding. If one of *my* daughters——"

"I suppose it is rather a queer proceeding ; but no doubt she gets tired of ' wasting her sweetness on the desert air' of Arling. Mind that you introduce me on the next opportunity, Aunt Mabel, or I vow I will never come and stay with you again."

Happily unconscious both of the admiration she had excited, and the criticism that had been passed on her conduct, Ida drove about the town in her gay reckless way, and transacted her shopping with her usual happy disregard of economy, paying for nothing, but contriving to run up one or two considerable bills.

She always enjoyed an expedition of this kind ; even the open-mouthed admiration of the young shopkeepers and clerks did not come amiss to her. Doubtless she would have preferred it if they had been young viscounts and earls, but, failing these, she applied the French proverb to her own case,

"Si l'on n'a pas ce qu'on aime,
Il faut aimer ce qu'on a."

It was surely better to be admired by an inferior class in the social scale than not to be admired at all.

At last she had accomplished all her business, and turned Dobbin's head towards home, giving him a touch of the whip, which caused the little animal to gambol and curvet in a way which showed that his spirit was by no means exhausted by his three hours' work.

Back again through the broad level country roads, deeply rutted by heavy carts and the pouring rain of the preceding day, in some places sparsely covered by the fallen leaves, blown down before their time by the boisterous autumnal winds.

It was nearly half-past twelve when they

left Daylesford, and Ida began to feel as if luncheon would be very acceptable——

Suddenly she caught sight of a gentleman walking on in front, dressed in a grey shooting jacket.

This apparition had the effect of making her draw the reins tighter, and reduce the pony's speed from a hand-gallop to a trot.

Surely there was only one man in or near Arling who walked at that free swinging pace, with upright *noble* figure, and shoulders well thrown back, his whole bearing that of an officer and a gentleman.

Yes, it was Captain Atherstone, and Ida's heart beat quickly as she saw him stop and turn round, his attention attracted by the sound of the pony's hoofs on the road.

He raised his hat as he caught sight of Ida, and would have walked on, but she stopped the little chaise, and leant down from her seat to shake hands.

"You are taking a long walk, Captain Atherstone; have you been into Daylesford?"

"Yes, I went to meet an old friend of

mine, but we missed somehow. What a
beautiful day, is it not, *Ida* ?"

"It is, *Arthur*."

They both laughed, and, leaning on the
side of the little carriage, the young man
glanced into her lovely flushed face, which
she averted as she said,

"Let me give you a lift home, you must
be very tired ."

He hesitated for a moment. Surely it
was rather a strange proposition. Anglo-
Indian young ladies often did such things,
but generally English ones were more particular.

Well, it was not his business to raise
objections which did not seem to occur to
her, so after that scarcely perceptible
moment of consideration, he gave a grateful assent, and took his place by Ida's side.

Away went Dobbin, at a good pace, but
not quite so fleetly as before. It was a
long drive, and doubtless Ida did not wish
to fatigue the poor pony ; as for her appetite, well, that was now quite a secondary
consideration.

Captain Atherstone leant back in his comfortable seat, and surveyed, with artistic appreciation, his companion's delicate complexion, the dark sweep of her eyelashes, and the thick bands of her waved golden hair, a little disordered now by the wind. But though there was much genuine admiration, there was no tender interest in the earnest gaze of his honest blue eyes; she was simply a beautiful girl to him, a clever girl, even an agreeable girl, but certainly not one to be loved, or even warmly esteemed.

With that native intuition which is almost a sixth sense with some women, Ida was perfectly aware of this, and yet she did not give up hope. She had a perfect and tranquil faith in the power of her own matchless beauty, and the difficulty of this pursuit only added to its zest.

After a few moments' silence, she opened the campaign, innocently enough.

"Do you think of remaining much longer at Arling?"

"My father leaves to-morrow. He would

have gone before, but the accounts of my
sister have been much more favourable of
late.   After all, the doctors thinks she may
get through the winter."

" I am so glad ; how you must be longing
to see her again."

" I am, indeed ; I wish I could start to-
morrow, but there is no hope of my being
able to get away this week."

He spoke warmly, and with undoubted
sincerity.

A shadow darkened the pretty face at his
side.

" And yet Arling is a very pleasant
place," she said softly.

" Very : I love every inch of the old
house, but of course Mary is more to me
than Arling.   But I shall always be glad
that we came here now (and he turned to
her with a pleasant smile).   It is so nice to
have known you both so well ; we are as
good friends as ever we were, are we
not ?"

Her answering smile was a little forced ;
she would have preferred a less open decla-

ration of his friendship. Men really in love are more reserved in their expressions.

"We are very glad to have renewed your acquaintance, Captain Athsertone," she said coldly, "though I dare say it will be another ten years before we meet again."

"*Captain Atherstone*, have you forgotten our compact?—don't let us get formal and tiresome again."

"*Arthur*, then, if you *really* prefer it."

"I do prefer it; we are such old friends, you know."

Ida almost stamped her foot; really this young man's persistent and obtuse friendliness was too provoking. But she only said,

"Is not Dobbin a duck of a pony?"

"He is very handsome, but, I should think, difficult to drive. I never saw a more excitable-looking little animal."

"What time is it?" asked Ida suddenly.

"Twenty minutes past one; are you late?" For she uttered a low exclamation, and gave Dobbin a touch of the whip, which urged him to the top of his speed.

" I must try and get well past the viaduct before the express passes," she said,
turning round her lovely flushed face.   " It
is due at the half-hour.   Just look along
the line, Arthur ; can you see anything of
it ?"

" Nothing at present.   Don't over-hurry
the poor little animal, Ida, you don't see
how hot he is getting."

She paid no attention, but touched Dobbin's sleek sides again and again with the
whip, till the excited animal flew along like
the wind.

Amid all her real anxiety she smiled to
herself at the considerable increase of intimacy which had been engendered by a
quarter of an hour's familiar and solitary
intercourse : it came naturally enough *now*
to say " Arthur " and " Ida."

Again Captain Atherstone leant back and
watched her set anxious face with a feeling of quiet amusement, for to his calm,
soldierly nature the danger appeared quite
imaginary.

But she was not mistaken.   Already in

the distance a faint whiff of smoke was apparent; it became more and more distinct; surely his watch was slow, or the express before its time—most likely the former.

On it came at lightning speed, rushing, panting, roaring, like some fabled monster of antiquity, the thundering noise grew louder and louder, and then——in despair, Ida pulled up short, perhaps the worst thing she could have done.

For one instant Dobbin stood perfectly still, shaking in every limb, then turning sharp round, with a few energetic kicks freed himself from the traces, and galloped back towards Daylesford, leaving the overturned carriage in the road with a broken shaft, but otherwise uninjured.

Captain Atherstone was pitched on his back in a muddy ditch half filled with water, but though soaked and dirtied from head to foot, he found himself uninjured by so much as a bruise.

His first thought was to look round for his fair charioteer.

5—2

She was lying in the road only a few feet from him, but even as he caught sight of her, she moved, and managed to struggle into a sitting posture.

"My dear Ida, are you hurt?" he exclaimed, hastening to her side.

She glanced up in his face, and much to his astonishment, and a little to his alarm, burst into a fit of laughter.

"Oh, Arthur! what have you done to yourself? you look like a tramp, your coat is all over mud, and your hat!"

He surveyed his dripping attire with a slight air of discomfiture ; no man likes to feel that he is presenting an absurd appearance, more especially in the eyes of a very pretty girl.

"I *do* look disreputable," he said ruefully ; "but upon my honour, Ida, you don't look much better—your hat seems to have disappeared altogether—oh, there it is !"

The unfortunate article was swimming in a large pool of rain water; and, as Arthur held it up, the soaked straw and straight dripping feather presented a very hopeless appearance.

" It is done for," said Ida, " and so is my jacket; oh, Arthur, how unfortunate we are! It is all the fault of your stupid watch" (with a sudden irresistible burst of temper).

" I am afraid it was, but it can't be helped now. It is a great mercy that neither of us are hurt ; are you *quite* sure you feel all right?"

She took his proffered arm, and rose to her feet, though with some difficulty.

" I don't think I am hurt, only I feel *awfully* stiff and bruised. Don't I look a fearful object, Arthur ?"

He glanced down at her white face and great blue appealing eyes, now fast filling with tears.

She had been brave enough at first, but the reaction was beginning, and her lips grew ashy and trembling, it was all she could do to stand.

" You *do* look rather bad," he said, compassionately ; "and the worst of it is, I don't know how on earth to get you home. You couldn't walk ?"—(very doubtfully).

"I suppose I could if I must. Oh, dear! how my shoulder aches!"

"Poor child! I am so sorry for you. Lean on me, Ida—your full weight—so. Good gracious! how white you look!"

Strange to say, as the gentleman's cheerfulness disappeared, the lady's courage rose visibly.

"I must try and walk home," she said. "It is nearly two miles, but I can do twice the distance any ordinary day. There is no chance of getting hold of that little beast, he will gallop right back to Daylesford." So they slowly advanced arm-in-arm, Ida carrying her crushed hat in her hand, her golden hair hanging rough and dishevelled, almost down to her waist.

Certainly some women are the better for a small misfortune of this kind, especially those who, as a rule, are rather masterful and imperious in manner. All Ida's high spirits had deserted her; she trudged along wearily, clinging fast to Arthur's arm, a

tired, draggled figure. All the smartness
and neatness of her appearance had gone,
but in his eyes she had never seemed so
fascinating. Could he but have had a
glimpse into her mind, he would have seen
that in spite of the gentle weariness of her
manner (caused by the late shock to her
system), her heart was beating high with
joy and triumph. Weeks of ordinary intercourse would not have brought them so
near together as the misfortune they had
mutually experienced. Surely it was well
worth while to have been overturned, even
at the risk of spoiling her best clothes and
losing her credit for good driving, for the
sake of this two-mile walk with Arthur,
during which he entirely laid aside any
previous coldness of manner, and was all
that is most kind and sympathizing.

Had Ida possessed but a little more in-
sight into character, she would have known
that this alteration was not of much real
signification as regarded her secret hopes.
Arthur Atherstone was a true gentleman
in every sense of the word ; he would have

assisted any aged woman or man who had met with an accident with exactly the same gentle solicitude which he was now bestowing on his beautiful companion. Still, it was a pleasant walk to both of them ; and perhaps Ida was not very far from the truth when, on safely reaching the Rectory, she congratulated herself on having advanced several degrees in her companion's liking and esteem. Captain Atherstone wisely refused to enter, and hastened on to the Grange to change his wet clothes. Ida paid very little attention to Elizabeth's exclamations and inquiries, and considerably astonished that kind sister by saying, as she rushed upstairs to her own room—

"You need not pity me in the least, I have been enjoying myself immensely. I only wish the same thing could happen every day."

"You *enjoyed* the accident !"

"Yes ; *enjoyed it immensely.*"

CHAPTER V.

"And Merlin looked, and half believed her true,
So tender was her voice, so fair her face,
So sweetly gleamed her eyes behind her tears,
Like sunlight on the plain behind a shower."

TENNYSON.

A DREARY, foggy day.

Captain Atherstone is sitting by himself in the Grange library, a large room, handsomely furnished, every article of the best manufacture, and elegant—even choice, of its kind, but it lacked that peculiar air of comfort and refinement which only feminine occupation can bestow.

Everything is in its place—the books arranged in martial order around the centre table, the newspapers carefully folded and laid in a pretty receptacle something like a toast-rack : in short, the genius of order seems to hold undisputed sway here not *tidiness,* which is always pleasant, but *order*—stern, unromantic, implacable *order.*

Arthur Atherstone is looking dull and dispirited to-day : perhaps he is thinking of the time when this silent room, now quiet and lonely as a vault, was alive with merry voices, when Lady Atherstone's sweet motherly influence pervaded the whole place, and his sisters' sunny faces and merry songs converted the dull old Grange into fairy-land. Ah, well! that happy time is gone for ever! Of those sweet sisters, one was lying in her lonely grave in Madeira ; the other was fast fading away from earth and all its cares and pleasures! A few short months, perhaps weeks, and of all that large and merry party, one only would remain !

" I—I only am left !" muttered the young man to himself as he rose from his seat and walked restlessly up and down the long room. "A strange fatality pursues my family.

Surely ere long it will overtake me as well as the others. I feel well and strong *now*, but no doubt I have the seeds of some incurable malady within me. Why should I escape more than they? With such an awful, certain, inevitable doom hanging over my head, I have no right to live as other men do—no right to cherish bright hopes or ambitious aspirations—no right *to marry!*"

At this stage of his melancholy reflections the door suddenly opened, and the butler announced—

" Lord Trevor."

In he came, a tall, handsome, dark young man. You have seen him once before, reader: he is the same who was driving through Daylesford in Mrs. Fletcher's carriage, and had been struck with admiration at sight of Ida Helmore.

Arthur advanced with outstretched hand.

" My dear Launcelot, where did you drop from? I had no idea you were in this part of the country."

" That is odd, my dear fellow, as you

made an appointment to meet me yesterday in Daylesford."

"To be sure I did; and I kept it, too.
It is very odd how we managed to miss each
other in such a small place. But I thought
you were only in Sussex for a couple of
hours on your way to London."

"That *was* my intention, but you see I
have altered it. I always was a changeable
fellow, you know; but this time I had good
reason for the change. We have been
friends for nearly twenty years, Arthur : I
am not going to let you make an important
change in your life without consulting me.
Don't imagine it. I have come in like the
disagreeable fatherly friend on the stage,
who always appears when he isn't wanted,
and intrudes his advice where it is not
required or expected."

"You are talking in riddles, Launcelot,
and I can't profess to understand you. I
am meditating no important change in my
life, unless it is the change through which
we must all pass—death."

"Nonsense, Arthur, don't be lugubrious.

Do you mean to say you really don't understand me ? or is it that you wish to keep the matter a secret ?" .

" On my word and honour I don't understand you."

" Well, you shall hear the whole story. I came to Daylesford yesterday morning, intending to spend a few hours with old Mother Fletcher : you remember her—the good old soul we always call Aunt Mabel, though she is only my mother's half-sister. We drove all over the place for about two hours, but could see nothing of you, so I yielded to my affectionate aunt's solicitations, and agreed to return home and spend some days with her, instead of proceeding to the great metropolis by the 5.15. I accepted her invitation, partly because I had caught sight of the most exquisite face I ever saw in the town, and—well, Arthur, I confess to you that for the time I was almost in love —almost, old fellow, not *quite*, so don't be jealous."

" Jealous ! what can it signify to me, except as it concerns you ?"

"It signifies a great deal to you, or ought
to do so. I little thought that my rustic
beauty would turn out to be *your* Miss
Helmore."

"What?"

"Ah! I have touched you at last, have
I? Well, in the course of our drive we
chanced to come upon a Miss Scarsdale
(one of the Daylesford aristocracy), and she
informed us, after a little adroit question-
ing on my part, that the golden-haired
beauty who was driving through the town
with such a charming air of independence
was Miss Ida Helmore, second daughter of
the Rector of Arling, and reported to be
your engaged wife."

"Launcelot, it is a falsehood—a bit of
abominable old maids' gossip. I am not
engaged to any girl on earth, nor am I
likely to become so."

"Then you must have been flirting *à
l'outrance.* Miss Scarsdale told us you
almost lived at the Rectory, and that when
you were not chatting with the girls you
were conversing on intimate terms with the

father. *That* looks suspicious, Arthur, you must allow. She finished by saying that no doubt your excuse of pressing business was a mere pretence to induce your father to allow you to remain on at Arling, and that probably your family would not cordially approve of the match."

"She is wrong there—they *would* approve of it; my father himself suggested it, but it is not likely to take place. I shall never marry, Launcelot."

Lord Trevor sat down opposite his friend, and gazed earnestly into his face.

"You are in low spirits, Arthur; don't deny it—I see you are."

"I do not attempt to deny it. Have I not cause? You know that Mary——"

"I know everything, my dear fellow; don't pain yourself by repeating it. Your family troubles have been, and are, very heavy, and I deeply sympathize with you on their account, but that is not what I am thinking of. It may be that your sister will not recover—though I hear she is much better; but what has that to do with your never marrying? Nothing at all; there is something else."

"There *is* something else. With our hereditary tendencies to disease, I have no right to link any woman's fate to mine. I——"

"Arthur, shall I tell you what is the matter with you?"

"Do."

"In one word, then, it is *fog*. You are not used to this dreary English autumn weather, and it depresses and enervates you; you are out of spirits, and therefore talk sentimental nonsense. You are no more likely to die prematurely than I am; and as for not having a right to 'link any woman's fate' to yours, the woman is much to be envied who secures you for a husband, though I wish—— Hullo! who's that?"

His lordship sprang from his seat and flew to the window, in time to catch sight of two young ladies who were walking quickly across the lawn.

"My rustic beauty herself! What an

unlucky fellow I am—always just too late
for everything! I say, Arthur, you couldn't
run after them, could you? I dare say
they wouldn't object to a cup of tea: I
believe women would drink tea at midnight
if they had the chance."

"I think they would be rather astonished
at the request," replied Arthur, smiling.
"They have leave to pass through our
grounds on their way home from the village
because it's a little shorter, but if they
were molested by us they would never
come again. Elizabeth Helmore is a particular young lady—very much so."

After a little more conversation, which
did not bear any direct reference to my
story, and therefore shall not be recorded
here, Lord Trevor took his leave, and
rode back to Daylesford, fully persuaded
that the report of his friend's engagement
was pure gossip, and therefore not worth
another serious thought. But the subject
was not so easily dismissed from Arthur
Atherstone's own mind. A more truthful,
conscientious, honourable character than his

never existed ; some men might have satisfied themselves with the consciousness that
they had never committed themselves by
word or deed, and that their conscience
was clear of any intention to deceive, but
he could not so quiet his mind. Certainly
he *had* been very often at the Rectory,
and was on most friendly and intimate
terms with the sisters, but surely they
must see how naturally it had come about.
A young man, living by himself in a dull,
empty house, within a stone's throw of two
pretty girls, is likely to find himself very
often in the society of those girls, especially
if they are old friends, and their's the only
gentleman's house within five or six miles.
Yet, if through any indiscretion of his
Ida's name had been compromised, *surely*
he owed her reparation.

But why had the gossiping tongues of
Daylesford selected *Ida* as the lady of his
supposed affections ? If anything, he had
paid more attention to Elizabeth. It was
all very annoying and perplexing, and
Arthur impatiently threw open the win-

dow and stepped out on the lawn, hoping
to compose his thoughts, and get rid of
the head-ache which was oppressing him
by a brisk walk in the chill autumn morning. How annoyed and disgusted would
he have been if the clue to the report of his
matrimonial engagement had been given
him, and he had traced it to its real source,
Ida herself, for such was the fact.

Ida's ambition and pride had suggested
to her a means of expediting her engagement with Arthur Atherstone by a few
judicious hints and innuendoes to some of
her Daylesford acquaintance, all done in a
quiet, ladylike manner, but distinctly con-
veying the impression to them that she was
being wooed, and might shortly be won.
Of course, it was merely a speculation, he
might never hear of it, but if he did (and
Ida depended greatly on the gossiping
propensities of the Daylesford ladies), then
it would be a powerful incitement to him
to propose to her. She reckoned on the
almost morbid sense of honour which was

one of Arthur's most striking characteristics, and she did not reckon in vain.

Before he returned from his walk that foggy autumn morning, Arthur Atherstone had decided that since he had been (however innocently) the cause of Ida's name being connected with his, it was his duty, as an officer and a gentleman, to give her the opportunity of accepting him as her husband. Perhaps, after all, she would refuse to marry him, and, if not—if *not*—well, there would be no harm done. Where, in broad England, would he find a wife so lovely, so accomplished, as Ida Helmore? If she had faults, they were but trivial defects, incidental to her age and circumstances—a motherless country girl has so few advantages. The cares and responsibilities of married life would sober her, and make her as faultless in mind as she was in person. And yet—and yet—in the dreams of a possible future married life, which had come to him as they come to all young men, it had not been of such a girl as Ida that he had thought. His ideal was a gentle, gracious woman, of perhaps two-and-twenty, with mild, loving eyes, and a low, persuasive voice—the voice which, as some writer has beautifully said, is best learnt by the cradles of little children. To his certain knowledge Ida hated children (never an amiable characteristic in a young woman), her lovely blue eyes were bright and expressive, but by no means soft, and her voice, though clear and gay, was very often the reverse of sweet.

After all his cogitations, Arthur felt very undecided, and at last he formed a resolution contrary to his usual energetic and decided character. He would do nothing hastily; he would wait the progress of events. He would watch Ida closely, and if he saw the smallest sign of real affection (in his humility he called it simply *prefer-ence*) for him, he would lay his hand and fortune at her feet. No man or woman should ever have the right to call him a flirt and a deceiver.

Poor Arthur Atherstone! he is not the first man who has been made the dupe of a fair, false woman, and has deemed himself the object of a pure and true affection, when all the time he is walking unsuspectingly into the snare laid for him by an artful and designing cupidity.

That afternoon old Mr. Helmore informed his eldest daughter that he intended to have a curate, and that a young Mr. Norman, from Oxford, had been suggested to him as one able and willing to undertake the post.

"I am glad to hear it, papa," replied Elizabeth. "Many people have told me that you ought to have had assistance long ago. This is a large and scattered parish, and some of our people have to be left unvisited, though I do what I can."

"I know you work hard, my dear, but I never see Ida assisting you in any way. She is old enough now to be of some use."

"She thinks she has no gift for conversing with poor people."

"It is a gift all may acquire. I fear she is getting to lead an idle, selfish life. You should see to it, Elizabeth; you stand in the place of a mother to her."

"I have often tried, dear papa, but Ida is a little difficult to manage, now she is no longer a child. I have very little control over her."

Mr. Helmore sighed, and walked to the window. Suddenly he gave a start, and exclaimed—

"Elizabeth, come here—quick! Is that Ida? Who is with her?"

She hastened to her father's side, and at once saw what his failing eyesight had but dimly distinguished. Ida was walking down the gravel path with Captain Atherstone; her arm was linked in his, and her beautiful face was upturned with a bright, sweet smile. They looked unmistakably a pair of lovers.

Mr. Helmore turned to his eldest daughter, and said, sternly—

"Is *this* the care you have taken of your sister?"

Elizabeth stood bewildered, her eyes filling with tears, her fair cheeks deeply flushed with mortification and annoyance. They were not kept long in suspense. Ida had dismissed Arthur at the gate leading into the lane, and, before her father and sister could say another word, she stood before them, looking more radiantly lovely than they had ever seen her, her eyes absolutely flashing with triumphant joy.

"Ida," began her father, "is this seemly conduct? Where have you been?"

"I have been in the garden all the afternoon, father."

"With Captain Atherstone?"

"With my affianced husband."

Mr. Helmore stood confounded, scarcely knowing whether to be most displeased or annoyed.

"You do not object, father?" said the young girl, anxiously. "It is a great match for me, you know."

· "God forbid that my daughter should marry for such a reason as that! My child, do you *love* him?"

One moment's hesitation, then she looked up half defiantly.

"What an old-fashioned idea, papa! Of course I shall love him—all wives love their husbands."

"Ah, dear! not all. Will you answer my question? I did not say, *Will* you love him, but *do* you love him?"

"Well, if it will satisfy you, yes—I—I do love him. Elizabeth, not a word from you! I thought you would be so pleased."

But Elizabeth had turned away with a heavy sigh. She had no congratulations to offer.

That evening, any curiosity which she might have felt was gratified, for Ida confided in her fully and freely. It seemed that she had gone into the garden that afternoon with no idea of meeting Arthur, but with the simple intention of bringing in some apples for dessert. He had accidentally caught sight of her from the road, and she had very naturally invited him to enter the garden and assist her to shake the trees.

"And then," continued Ida, kneeling at

her sister's feet in their own little bedroom,
"then, Elizabeth, while we were talking he
looked into my face and said, quite suddenly, that he was going away, that his
business at Arling was all but finished, and
that by this time to-morrow he hoped to be
at Torquay. I did not know what to say;
my heart seemed to stop beating—it was
so sudden, so *dreadful*. After all my plans
and hopes, that he should be taking leave
of me in that heartless, commonplace manner, as if we were only ordinary acquaintances. What do you think I did, Elizabeth?"

"Said good-bye and wished him a pleasant journey, of course."

"You dear old prosaic thing. No, I did
nothing of the sort. I just turned away
my head and burst out crying."

"Ida, Ida, how could you betray yourself so!"

"Wait a bit. You will be more shocked
before I have done. Well, when he saw I
was crying, he bent down, and took one of
my hands in his, and said, so gently and

kindly, 'Does my going away make you so unhappy, Ida?' and I replied, 'I never was so miserable in my life!' So he was silent for a moment, and then he said, 'You shall not be made unhappy, Ida; if you really love me, dear, why should we not be married, and never separated again? *Will* you be my wife?' And I said something —I don't quite know what it was, but it meant *Yes*, and he understood me."

" Was that all, Ida ?"

" That was all."

" Not a word of *his* love for *you* ?"

" Not a word; I did not expect it. Why, Elizabeth, he does not care much about me, I know that; but he will—wait a few weeks, and you will see."

" But I can't understand, dear, if he does not love you, why did he ask you to marry him ?"

" Oh! I don't know; he is a very honourable man, and all that sort of thing; and you see he *has* been a good deal here, and people are beginning to talk ; besides,

he thinks I adore him.   Oh dear! oh dear!
what geese men are !"

"You are a strange girl, Ida!   How can
you bear to contemplate the life which lies
before you—a life spent with a man who
does not care for you, and who only proposed to you from a feeling of duty and
honour !   I cannot——"

"Oh ! don't preach, Elizabeth.   I know
all you have to say, and I am sure it is
very reasonable and right; but it is of no
use to argue with me.   My mind is fully
made up ; 1 am sick of Arling and all its
surroundings : if I do not marry I shall
run away or do something eccentric which
will shock you all.   Believe me, I know
what is best for myself."

"But is it best for *him*?"

Elizabeth had moved to the window-
seat, and sat there, her face turned away
from the lighted room, looking out on the
still September night.

"Do not think worse of me than I de-
serve," said Ida, in a lowered voice.   "I
know you think me deceitful, and am-

bitious, and scheming, and everything that is bad; but indeed, *indeed*, Elizabeth, I mean to make him love me—I mean to try and make him happy. I believe I am one of those persons who can be very good and kind if they have their own way, but a disappointment would have soured me for life. I have *not* been disappointed; everything has turned out well and happily, so you need not fear for me, Elizabeth. I shall be a model wife, and Arthur will be the happiest of husbands!"

Elizabeth made no reply, and feeling chilled and hurt, Ida turned away, and began brushing her hair vehemently. Had she been a little closer to her sister, she would have seen that her features, ordinarily so calm, were now working with suppressed feeling, her very lips were white, and the soft grey eyes were brimming over with tears. Only for a few minutes, however; her habitual self-command soon came to her aid, and when she turned again to the light, no trace of unusual emotion was visible in her sweet face. She then crossed the room and kissed Ida, who was sitting reading on her bed.

"Forgive me if I have seemed unsympathizing, dear," she said, kindly; "it is all so very sudden, and—and—I have not got quite used to the idea. But I do congratulate you—I congratulate you with all my heart."

Ida looked up in surprise: the tone was so constrained, the words so set and conventional, altogether so unlike Elizabeth— what *had* come to her? She had no opportunity of inquiring, for Elizabeth had quickly turned away, and, taking a prayer-book from the table, began her evening reading with an air which showed she did not wish to be disturbed. So Ida wondered on. Perhaps some light would have been thrown on her perplexity if she had overheard the words which her sister constantly murmured during her restless night—

"If she had only loved him I could have borne it! but she does not—it is only to get away from home. I might have made her happier. Oh, Ida, Ida!"

Vain reproaches! and as undeserved as vain!

CHAPTER VI.

"If to her share some female errors fall,
   Look in her face, and you'll forget them all."

POPE.

THOSE of my readers who have accompanied me thus far will probably imagine that the plot of this story is now plain, if indeed they had not guessed it from the first. Of course, as time went on, Arthur became aware of the unworthy part Ida had taken to promote her own hasty and ill-advised engagement, and equally, of course, he became persuaded of the superior excellence of Elizabeth's character, and ended by marrying her and freeing himself from the shackles which had been unfairly riveted upon him. Nothing of all this took place.

Contrary to all the rules of poetical justice, Ida's deceit prospered better even than she could have expected : not only did Arthur never discover that his keen sense of honour had been taken advantage of, but in the course of a very few days his lingering doubts entirely disappeared, and he began to be thoroughly happy in his engagement.

The accounts of his sister continued so satisfactory, that he determined to remain a fortnight longer at Arling before returning to his expectant family at Torquay. During these last days Ida brought into play all the wonderful attractive power of which she was possessed, in order to win the heart of her somewhat apathetic lover. She succeeded beyond even her most sanguine hopes.

Gradually Arthur began to change the opinion which he had at first conceived of her character ; she was so gentle, so considerate always of his feelings and his convenience, all the old coquetry and wilfulness was laid aside, and with it that gay, flighty manner

which at one time had almost disgusted
him.

Ida was not altogether acting a part.
She had spoken the simple truth when she
had told her sister that she was one of those
persons who are much improved by pros-
perity. She was thoroughly happy now
all the old discontent and weariness of
life had passed away; she had a bright
future before her, and the consciousness of
this made her gracious and sweet to every
one.

Arthur Atherstone was not an exigeant
lover, but he was a very attentive one.
He showered magnificent and costly presents on his betrothed; he was at her beck
and call all hours of the day; and his manner to her was marked by a gentle, chivalrous courtesy, which would have soon won
the hearts of most girls.

Elizabeth watched her sister closely, and
tried hard to make herself believe that the
affection which had certainly been wanting
before her engagement was wakening into
life now. But she could not persuade her-

self that such was the case ; many small, but significant, circumstances went to disprove it. When a handsome gold locket, enriched with splendid rubies and pearls, was sent to Ida from Arthur, she gazed at it and toyed with it for a whole morning, but she let his photograph lie neglected for an entire week on a table in her own room, scarcely taking the trouble to glance at it, till one morning Elizabeth saw it lying on the floor, and put it carefully away. Most girls treasure up their love-letters ; Ida tore hers up, or threw them carelessly behind the grate.

Strange to say, of all the parties concerned, Mr. Helmore was the only one who expressed any outward dissatisfaction with the engagement. Both Sir Henry and Lady Atherstone wrote kind, affectionate letters to the young couple, expressing their warm approval of the attachment, and thus giving a proof of the loving, unworldly spirit which prompted them to sanction their only son's engagement with the penniless daughter of a country clergyman.

But though he was grateful for their kindness, and to a certain extent flattered by his daughter's conquest, good old Mr. Helmore's mind was not at ease. Perhaps the ill-success of his own matrimonial venture had made him a little over cautious, and imparted a tinge of suspicion to his otherwise candid and genial nature.

"I fear the marriage will not turn out happily," he said one day to Elizabeth; "her heart is not in it."

"I think he is very much attached to her," was the answer, "and love begets love."

"His attachment must be of very recent date; I saw no signs of it a week ago."

"Let us hope they know what is best for their happiness, dear papa. I do really think that Ida is very much improved by her engagement; she is more gentle and steady than she ever was before."

The conversation dropped, but neither party felt really convinced or satisfied. Three days before Arthur's departure he received a note from Lord Trevor, which ran as follows :—

    " DEAR ARTHUR,

        What an astonishing fellow you are. So you were trying to hoodwink me when I called at Arling, and saw your fair inamorata crossing the lawn, and you swore you had no idea of making her an offer. I think you might have confided in me; indeed I don't understand now why you did not. All I can say is that if your indifference was all acting, it was uncommonly well done; and if it was genuine, your love is the fastest-growing plant I ever heard of—Jonah's gourd is a fool to it. Write directly and explain it all, for I never felt so puzzled in my life.

                " Yours ever,

                    " TREVOR."

It is unnecessary to say that Arthur *did* not write directly, and when at last he set himself to reply, the letter was not one exactly calculated to satisfy his friend's curiosity. It only consisted of two or three lines.

"DEAR TREVOR,

"You should know enough of me by this time to be sure that I did not attempt to 'hoodwink' you the day·you came here. I did *not* care for Ida Helmore then, nor had I any thoughts of making her my wife. Don't ask for explanations. I am now perfectly happy and satisfied, and am convinced that I shall never regret the choice I have made.

"Yours sincerely,

"A. ATHERSTONE."

Now that she had safely hooked her fish, Ida was naturally impatient to complete the business, and land him high and dry in the matrimonial basket. Indeed, there was no reason for delay, and it was finally settled that if Miss Atherstone's health continued to improve, the wedding should take place early in November.

The day that Arthur was obliged to

leave Arling, Ida gratified him considerably by proposing to walk with him to the station, though his train left at eight o'clock, and as a rule she hated early rising. It was a fine morning, bright and mild, and the young betrothed looked as fresh and sweet as a rose, as she walked down the lane to meet Arthur at his own gate.

"You are punctual, darling," he said, as he came to meet her. "Do you know, I had my doubts if, after all, you would summon resolution to get up in time."

"It is a very small sacrifice to make for you, Arthur," she replied, looking up in his face with a smile; "and who knows how long it may be before I shall have a chance of another walk with you."

"Not many days, I hope. If Mary is really so much better, I may even be back before the end of this week."

"If you think so, why go at all ?"

"Because I cannot rest satisfied without seeing her. She is the most unselfish girl in the world. Even now I do not know that she may not have been persuading my mother to keep the worst from me, for fear I should hurry away from you for her sake."

" I think you are very fond of your sister, Arthur."

" Certainly I am ; are you not fond of Elizabeth ?"

" Yes, of course, but not, I think, quite in the same way. I would not be hurried away from *you* for twenty Elizabeths."

" My dear Ida, do not speak in that reproachful way. Do you not see that I *must* go ?"

" No doubt you think you must. Here we are ; what a short walk it has seemed. You must make haste, Arthur; the five minutes' bell has rung."

A hasty dash into the office for his ticket, a glance to assure himself that the cart with the luggage had arrived safely, and he was again at her side.

" One word, Ida, the train is just in sight. My darling, I want you to promise me *one* thing, will you ?"

" Anything, dear Arthur—anything."

" Don't drive alone into Daylesford, especially on a market-day. You are not offended, dear? It is only a fancy of mine."

"It *is* rather absurd, Arthur; but I promise."

" Thank you, dear. Write often to me, Ida."

" I will answer every one of your letters, but I warn you, I am a very bad letter-writer. Good-bye, Arthur."

The train came puffing and roaring into the little station, and in another minute was slowly winding its long length out again. Ida stood and watched it till the last whiff of smoke disappeared into the tunnel, and then turned and walked home slowly, thinking to herself, " I was certainly born under a lucky star. How handsome he looked this morning, and how affectionate he was to me. I do believe that he has *set himself* to care for me with his whole heart and soul, just because he thinks it is his duty, and he will never rest till he *has* given me his whole heart." She was quite right.

Let the scene change to the drawing-room of the little house at Torquay, where Lady Atherstone and her daughter Mary are awaiting the arrival of the much-loved and only son. Lady Atherstone is standing by the window, a handsome, matronly figure still, though age and many sorrows have silvered her dark hair, and a little dimmed the brightness of her loving blue eyes. Her features are regular and noble in outline, and her hands remarkably delicate and beautiful. There is about her that peculiar charm which can only be possessed by one who unites the gentle, dignified composure of a perfectly well-bred woman, with all the loving warmth of a most tender and unselfish mother. Close to her, on a sofa, lies her daughter Mary, a young woman of perhaps four or five and twenty. There is the pallor of incurable ill-health on her thin cheek, but it is a pleasant face to look at still. There is much of her mother's peculiar grace and refinement about her small, regular features, and she has that great and rare charm in a woman, a very low, sweet-toned voice.

" He is late, mamma," she says. " Did he not promise to be here to luncheon ?"

" He will not fail, darling; I never knew Arthur to break his word. Ah ! there he is !"

A fly drove up, and the light, active figure they knew so well jumped out, and in another minute was embracing his mother and sister. .

" My dear boy, we thought you were *never* coming back to us," said Lady Atherstone, holding his hand in hers, and looking at him in the peculiar adoring, satisfied way that mothers have.

" Dear mother, you know——"

" Yes, Arthur, we did not expect you," said Mary, smiling up at him. " I .think it was very good of you to come at all."

" Shall you be able to stay now ?—No, I suppose we ought not to expect that," said Lady Atherstone, a little anxiously.

" I will stay till Mary is better," he replied, seating himself by her side. " You are not looking quite strong yet, dear sis."

After a little more conversation Lady

Atherstone left the room, thinking, in her unselfishness, that no doubt the brother and sister would like to be alone for a time. Then Mary nestled closer to her brother's side, and said—

"Now, Arthur, tell me all about *her*."

He straightway launched into a description of Ida, and became both enthusiastic and poetical in his word-painting, but his sister listened almost with impatience.

"But, dear Arthur," she said at last, "I want to know more about *her*. You tell me she has golden hair and a lovely complexion, and beautiful eyes, but is she a girl I can love? Will she, in any way, take the place of a sister to me? Is she gentle and unselfish, like dear Blanche?"

Arthur hesitated. It was easier to give an inventory of Ida's personal charms than to dilate upon the excellences of her character. Could he, in truth, say that she was *gentle* and *unselfish*? was she really in any way like his dead sister, whom he remembered as the best and sweetest girl he had ever known?

Mary began to fear she had been indiscreet as the minutes passed on, and he made no reply.

"Perhaps she is not quite that sort of girl," she said at last, anxiously ; "perhaps she is very strong-minded, and clever and——"

"No, she is not *that*," he replied, hastily. "I scarcely know what to say about her character, Mary, you see, we have been engaged such a very short time. I think you will like her. She is very bright and amusing, and such an exquisite face. There were some pretty English girls in Bombay, but I never saw one the least like her," etc., etc.

Mary had turned away her face, and lay looking out on the still, blue sea, an anxious expression on her face, that a little marred its gentle sweetness. She had every wish to be pleased and satisfied, but she could not help feeling a little puzzled.

All this talk about personal appearance was very unlike Arthur; he had always said that he would never marry a beauty, and yet he seemed to have engaged himself to a girl whose sole attraction lay in her good looks, and in being bright and amusing.   It was *not* quite satisfactory.

At this moment Sir Henry entered the room, and greeted his son with much affection.

"So, my boy, you took my advice after all," he said, in his happy, genial way; "depend upon it, the old folks are generally right in the end.   Mary, my dear, your brother is going to give you a sister-in-law, who will be an honour to the family. You are a lucky fellow, Arthur, though the girl has not a farthing.   I had rather you married a daughter of my old friend Helmore than any heiress in London."

Here Lady Atherstone returned, and the conversation became general.   Only Mary lay silently back on her sofa, feeling wholly unable to join in the merry talk, not only from physical weakness, but from mental depression.   That feeling of undefined anxiety and apprehension as regarded her brother's marriage was very strong upon her, and it grew heavier each day of Arthur's visit.

Was it in truth only the nervous fancy of an invalid girl, or was it that marvellous clearness of perception, almost amounting to prophecy, which is sometimes given to the dying, and which weighed upon her constantly, urging her to warn this dear brother against a marriage which would bring him no happiness. For she *was* dying—in spite of the doctor's cheering opinion, in spite of the renewed hope of those around her, in spite of the very decided improvement in her health, she never lost the conviction that Death was near at hand. He might be delayed for a time, but his stealthy footsteps never faltered, never turned back—she was doomed to die as her sisters had died—suddenly, painlessly —just when their recovery had been pronounced possible, and even probable !

Mary *knew* this, but Arthur never suspected this. Those days at Torquay passed away very peacefully and pleasantly : in after years Arthur looked back on them as the happiest time in his life.

Lady Atherstone once proposed that Ida should be asked to visit them, but he did not second the motion, and she was only too glad to have her son to herself. Arthur felt that it might be as well that his family should not see very much of his young betrothed till they were actually married. Ida was everything that was lovely, and charming, and affectionate, but she was not the least like the Atherstones; her innocent gaiety would seem like frivolity to *them*, their calm, quiet, gentle ways would appear cold and uninteresting to *her*.

"If it had been Elizabeth," argued Arthur with himself, "she might have come to us, and I know my mother would soon have loved her; but Ida is so very different— I don't think even Mary would have appreciated her."

No doubt he was right.

CHAPTER VII.

"And yet believe me, good as well as ill,
Woman's at best a contradiction still."
                                        POPE.

THE evening before her wedding-day Ida was sitting by herself in their little bed-room. Elizabeth was engaged in many household matters, and her father was in the parish, so there was nothing to disturb the young bride, and she had remained in that pleasant window-seat alone for nearly an hour.

Everything around bore tokens of the important event that was to take place on the morrow. On the bed lay the wedding-dress, a sheeny, glossy heap of white satin, tiny bunches of orange-blossom showing

here and there; a few half-packed boxes
and bags littered the usually tidy little
rooom—not *many*, for the country clergyman's second daughter could not afford
the magnificent and extensive trousseau
that most young ladies consider an indispensable part of their marriage arrange-
ments.   Neither were there many wedding
presents.   Sir Henry Atherstone had sent
her a handsome pearl necklace, which Lady
Atherstone had supplemented with a tiara,
bracelets, and earrings en suite.   Mary
Atherstone had given a pretty gold and
ruby bracelet, and Mrs. Fletcher a set of
pink coral.   This was nearly all, except a
few trifling souvenirs from old friends in
the village—"little and good," as Ida had
laughingly remarked the day before.

The wedding was to be quite private—
not even a breakfast.   Ida was to change
her dress immediately after they returned
from the church, and in half-an-hour's time
they were to be en route for Folkestone.
There was to be no foreign tour—Ida did
not care for it, and Arthur was glad to be

saved the necessity of going far from home while his sister continued in so precarious a state.

He had now arrived at Arling, but Ida had, somewhat to his surprise, refused to see him the day before the wedding. "We shall see enough of each other afterwards," she had said, half laughing, half wearily, to her sister. So Arthur had taken a long, solitary ramble on the downs, and Ida sat in her own little room alone.

Well, she has succeeded in her expectations, she is on the very eve of grasping all she has most longed for—ease, luxury, wealth, and a young, loving, and handsome husband to boot. Yet she does not look absolutely happy. There is an anxious look on her fair young face as she leans out of the open casement, heedless of the damp November evening air. Her pretty slender fingers are nervously clenched, and she has drawn off her diamond engaged ring, and thrown it half impatiently on the dressing-table.

Hitherto we have shown only the darkest

side of Ida Helmore's character; but she was not really a bad girl—not worse than many others who hold a fair position in the world, and are much loved and esteemed. Her faults were all *young* faults, such as are common to many a beautiful girl. She was a little frivolous, a little selfish, and *not* a little ambitious.

Ah! there it was. She had allowed herself to indulge discontented thoughts, till her present mode of life, from being only uncongenial, had become simply intolerable; and she was prepared to do, say, or suffer anything that might procure her a release from it. Had she failed, she might have been a soured, discontented, unamiable woman for life; but, having succeeded, softer and wiser thoughts began to pass into her mind.

A really religious education is never quite lost—really good seed can never be utterly fruitless. Looking back on her past life, she began to see how peaceful and sheltered it had been, how happy it *ought* to have been. What a kind father she had

possessed! what a loving, devoted sister!
And Arling itself—what a sweet, healthy
spot it was! what a warm, cosy nest was
this parsonage home of theirs! how beautiful the view from the windows! how pure
and invigorating the fresh breezes from the
Down! Yes, it was all very delightful,
and it was fast drawing to a close! A few
more hours, and she would have left this
quiet spot, and the peaceful life of the
daughter of an English country clergyman,
and entered upon the more brilliant, but
perhaps less safe, career of a married lady
of wealth, position, and fashion.

Ida did not, at any rate in these last
moments, attempt to deceive herself. She
did not love her handsome, chivalrous lover;
she had used him as the indispensable means
to a desired end; she admired and respected
him, but of that warm affection which a
good wife should bear to a loving husband
she knew that her heart was wholly empty.

"But I will try to love him—I will try
hard," she murmured to herself; "and
surely I must succeed. He is so good, and

so fond of me, surely it cannot be very difficult."

Ah, Ida! love is too brave and hardy a plant to flourish in the heated atmosphere of a forcing-house. It must be shone upon by the bright sun of heaven and nourished by its dews, pure breezes of reciprocal affection and kind deeds and words must constantly refresh it, and in such an atmosphere

"They sin who tell us love can die."

But like the little blue speedwell of the Sussex lanes, love will spring here and there at its own sweet will, rejecting a cultivated soil, and punishing every interference with its freedom by a premature withering and decay. It must be a peculiarly noble nature that, having withheld its best affection during the illusive season of courtship, will bestow them after the grave and unromantic realities of marriage.

Arthur Atherstone had no such misgivings on the eve of *his* wedding-day.

When not depressed by the thought of the dismal fate that seemed to pursue his family, his was a singularly bright and hopeful nature, disposed to make the best of everything and think the best of everybody. He looked forward with confidence to a life of much happiness spent with his young wife : her exquisite beauty and winning ways had completely taken possession of his heart, and he deemed himself the most fortunate man in England. He would now have rejected the faintest shadow of a doubt as to her love for him, or as to the perfect simplicity and beauty of her character, as an unworthy and dishonourable feeling, to be suppressed without a moment's hesitation. In a few brief hours she would be his—his own beautiful, peerless Ida—a treasure to be guarded carefully, and cherished most tenderly, till death should part them.

The short November day ended at last, and Ida was obliged to leave her quiet retreat, and come downstairs to the last dinner she was ever destined to eat in Arling Rectory.

They spent a very quiet evening. Mr. Helmore tried hard to talk and be cheerful, but *made* conversation is seldom a success, and by degrees they all relapsed into silence. Neither did the sisters talk much when they were alone in their own room that night. Elizabeth moved quietly about, gathering up small forgotten odds and ends, and closing bags and boxes with her usual neat dexterity, but it was all done very silently.

When all was finished, she came close to her sister's bedside, and bent down to say the last good-night. Ida's arms folded round her neck in a close, tight embrace, which seemed as if it never would unclose; and when, at last, Elizabeth gently drew herself away, she found the front of her dress wet with tears. She deemed it wiser not to notice this, but she tenderly smoothed the fair, ruffled hair with her motherly hand, and, by sundry loving, soothing words, showed the sisterly sympathy she scarcely dared to express openly.

After all, it was not unnatural; many girls were low and depressed on the point of leaving old friends and associations for ever. It may be doubted whether *any* girl feels cheerful on the eve of her wedding-day, though she may have every reason to look forward to a bright future.

So argued Elizabeth, sensibly enough no doubt, but she failed to convince herself, and, in spite of all her endeavours, the morning of that memorable 8th of November found her nervous and depressed. The weather was not inspiriting : a dense fog in the early morning changed about ten o'clock to a dreary, mizzling rain, and there was some difficulty in getting the bride dry to church. She was obliged to walk some few steps, and so damp was the atmosphere, that even in that moment the fog hung in heavy drops from her hair, and the lace veil drooped limp and flabby.

To Elizabeth it all seemed like some strange, awful dream. The gaslights, burning yellow and dim through the thick atmosphere, her father's surpliced form, less erect than usual, as he pronounced the solemn, unaccustomed words; Arthur's flushed, handsome face, brighter than ever from the contrast of the gloom around; and the bride's graceful, bending figure, looking almost unearthly with her gleaming hair and set, white face.

Could that indeed be her own sister ?— she who had been her constant companion day and night for eighteen years—that stately lady in the flowing satin dress and wreath of orange-blossom, who was now listening so intently to the exhortation which commanded her to be a follower of all " holy and godly matrons ?"   It was all *most* strange, *most* unnatural.

With the same dreamy feeling Elizabeth followed the married couple into the vestry, and mechanically kissed her sister, and received Arthur's warm shake of the hand.

Luncheon was ready in the dining-room when they returned—too simple a repast to be dignified by the name of a breakfast, but distinguished by a certain grace and fitness which characterized all Elizabeth's undertakings.

Ida had barely time to change her dress and swallow a few mouthfuls of food, when the carriage drove to the door, and they had to hurry away to catch the train for Folkestone. A few minutes of bustle and agitation, a momentary embrace of the bride in her rich dark blue silk and white bonnet—and they were off!

Elizabeth stood in the porch, heedless of the misty, drenching rain, watching the Atherstone carriage with its four greys, till it faded into a mere dot along the broad turnpike road. Then she went back into the drawing-room, and, sitting down on Ida's favourite sofa by the window, strove to collect her scattered senses.

"Married and done for," "wooed and married and a'"—how common are such sentences, and yet how untrue. If a girl is married at all, the event generally takes place before she is thirty, often before she

is five-and-twenty, with all the best years
of her life before her, containing all their
limitless possibilities of joy and sorrow,
well-doing and sin. Do not the real records
of a life begin when in novels they most
frequently end, when the bride has signed
her maiden name for the last time, and
the wedding-bells have ceased to clash
through the air?

How merciful is the veil which hides from
us not only our own future, but the future
of those dearest to us! Poor Elizabeth,
sitting there in her desolation, trying hard
to rouse herself from her despondency with
thoughts of comfort and hope! Could she
but have had but one glimpse of the future
which lay before that fair young bride,
would she not have striven desperately to
recall her? would she not have invented
any pretence, *any* excuse, which might
serve to avert, or at any rate postpone,
the inevitable hand of destiny?

But she knew nothing—foreboded nothing; and when at last she went to seek
her father in his study, she found him

composed and cheerful. Any misgivings that he might have had as to the prudence of the marriage were at an end now, and his usual peaceful serenity had returned to him.

CHAPTER VIII.

"But all my heart is drawn above ;
    My knees are bowed in crypt and shrine ;
  I never felt the kiss of love,
    Nor maiden's hand in mine."
                              TENNYSON.

THE morning after Ida's wedding rose clear, cold, and beautiful. Elizabeth determined to take a long walk to see some cottagers at the far end of the village, partly for the exercise and partly to fulfil a charitable purpose; partly, also, in the hope that a brisk walk in the frosty air might do something to remove the feeling of languor and depression that hung over her. In her neat black hat, waterproof cloak, and comfortable strong boots, she looked every inch the good, useful, clergyman's daughter, and the country people turned as she passed, and blessed the calm, sweet face that always seemed like a messenger of comfort to them.

No busy, useful person who has good health and a clear conscience, can remain long depressed, and Elizabeth felt her spirits rise as she stepped quickly along the hard road, and long before she had gone a couple of miles, she was disposed to see everything in a more cheerful light; even the lonely life spent in an obscure village which she imagined lay before her. " I shall never marry," she mused to herself; "it is most unlikely that I shall ever see any one to care for me in Arling; and it is just as well, for, after all, I believe old maids are the most contented people in the world. I shall have enough to do for the present in looking after papa, and helping in the parish, and by-and-by I shall be the useful, comfortable maiden aunt to Ida's children. Dear Ida ! I wonder what she is doing now ? I wonder——"

But her meditations were here cut short

by an unexpected sight on the road before her. Two gentlemen were walking slowly along side by side; one was Mr. Helmore, the other a tall young man, in clerical costume. Surely it could be no other than the new curate. He had not been expected until the next day, but no doubt something had occurred to induce him to alter his plans.

Mr. Helmore stopped when he saw Elizabeth, and introduced the stranger to her, adding—

"I met Mr. Norman walking from the station, my dear, and we are going to take a turn round the village. Are you going far?"

"Only to Deanworth, papa. I want to see those poor Watsons."

"You must be a good walker," said the curate, smiling; "Deanworth is nearly four miles from here."

"I believe it is quite that. Do you know this part of the country?"

"I have visited Daylesford once or twice."

"You must not delay, Elizabeth, or you will not be back to luncheon," said her father ; and the gentlemen walked on, and were soon out of sight,

Elizabeth hurried on, but she was not destined to reach Deanworth that morning. At the turn of the road she encountered Mrs. Fletcher's well-appointed carriage, and the good lady stopped at once and entered into conversation.

"My dear Elizabeth, I was just coming to the Rectory. How fortunate to have met you. Where are you going?"

"To Deanworth, dear Mrs. Fletcher. I am so sorry that I cannot stop, but it is a long way, and——"

"My dear girl, it is absurd : you will never get there. These bright mornings are not trustworthy. Look at that bank of clouds coming up with the wind ; there will be a drenching shower presently."

"I have a parcel to leave, and with my waterproof cloak——"

"I will leave your parcel as I drive

home ; it will not be ten minutes out of my way. Jump in, Elizabeth, like a good girl, and I will drive you back."

She was so earnest that Elizabeth allowed herself to be persuaded, and in another minute they were swiftly rolling back to Arling.

" Now, my dear," began the elderly lady, " tell me all the news. How did the wedding go off? Of course our dear little bride looked beautiful."

" She did, indeed. It was a pity the day was so gloomy. Everything looked so drenched and wretched."

" Of course, people who want sunny weather mustn't be married in November. I have loads of things to ask you, Elizabeth, but of course I shall forget half of them. Are you quite satisfied with the marriage, dear? Was it *really* and *truly* a love-match ?"

Elizabeth felt the question somewhat impertinent, but nevertheless she would have given worlds to have been able to answer it satisfactorily. Her momentary hesitation did not escape her companion's watchful eye.

" People have been saying that the engagement took place very soon after they became acquainted—*very* soon indeed, but of course there has been time since then for the young people to know each other thoroughly."

" I wish ¿people' would mind their own business," replied Elizabeth, with a sort of weary irritation.

This conversation was bringing back the anxious, doubtful feelings which had been partially dispelled by her long walk.

Mrs. Fletcher looked wise, and nodded indescribable things.

" Well, my dear, I won't press you; we must hope it will all turn out for the best. To change the conversation, how do you like the notion of a curate coming to Arling?"

" He has come already; he arrived unexpectedly this morning."

" Indeed! He must be a zealous young disciple. I know a little about him. The

Normans are a very good Hampshire family, and this young man ought to have money. He is the eldest son, is he not?"

"I don't know, indeed; I have made no inquiries."

"Just like you, Elizabeth; you always were the most inconsiderate young person about these matters. Have you not thought that a possibility exists of this young man taking a fancy to you? *Possibility!* I may almost call it a certainty; he will see no one else, and most curates have a genius for marrying. If you have no idea of his future prospects, how are you to answer when he makes you an offer?"

Elizabeth smiled.

"Our new curate is a High Churchman, Mrs. Fletcher and papa say, and is particularly averse to the society of young ladies. I very much doubt if I shall ever interchange a word with him except an occasional greeting, which I suppose we cannot well avoid."

"'When I said I should die a bachelor, I did not think I should live till I were married,'" quoted Mrs. Fletcher, laughing. "Never despair, Elizabeth, the most determined anchorites are conquered at last. Rely on it, I shall congratulate you as Mrs. Norman before next year closes."

"Indeed, I assure you——"

"There, there, my dear, that will do; I know what you are going to say. All young ladies think it necessary to make affirmations of perpetual celibacy, but there is not one who would refuse a good offer if she could get it. When I was a girl, I scouted the idea of matrimony as much as any of you, but it was a different thing when Mr. Fletcher proposed to me. You have no mother, Elizabeth—more's the pity—but you may always confide in *me*."

It was useless to reply, and Elizabeth leant back silently in her seat, and felt considerably relieved when they reached the Rectory gate; and Mrs. Fletcher, declining to enter, drove away with the parcel 'for Deanworth.

Mr. Helmore met his daughter in the porch.

"I have asked Mr. Norman to stay to luncheon, Elizabeth ; they did not expect him at his lodging, and nothing was prepared."

"Very well, papa ; I will see about it."

She gave the necessary directions to the cook, and soon appeared in the drawing-room, where she found the curate engaged in what was apparently a very interesting discussion with her father. He was so absorbed that she could watch his countenance without risk of observation, as she sat working on Ida's sofa.

He was certainly a very handsome man, though he had nothing of the rosy English comeliness which made Arthur Atherstone's face such a pleasant one to look at. On the contrary, his form was thin almost to meagreness, his large blue eyes were unusually bright and keen ; and his high, pale forehead and emaciated features, regular and handsome as they undoubtedly were, gave one the impression of very delicate health.

All sorts of comparisons flitted through

Elizabeth's mind as she watched him ; but perhaps the one which remained longest and made deepest impression on her mind was that of St. Augustine.

As she entered the drawing-room he was speaking earnestly and rapidly.

" Rely on it, Mr. Helmore, the extreme Ritualists are doing us good service. Romantic and wavering enthusiasts are led by them to forsake our Church for the Romish Communion — their natural and proper place ; *we* are glad to get rid of them, and they are welcomed *there.* I am convinced that many good persons make themselves very uneasy about the present state of ecclesiastical matters without the smallest occasion. Never has our Church been so flourishing or so useful, never has her influence been so widely spread or so universally acknowledged as in the present day."

" A house divided against itself falleth," replied Mr. Helmore, sadly. " I cannot but regret all these dissensions ; the spirit of Christian charity seems far enough removed from us at present. Fifty years ago, when I first entered the ministry, there were even those who entertained hopes of uniting the Nonconformists to our Church by means of a few simple and unimportant concessions; but what man in his senses would dream of such a ₍thing now? Disputes and discord are the order of the day. Look at the disgraceful scenes that are witnessed even at our Church Congresses."

"Fifty years ago, sir," replied the young man with animation —"fifty years ago there were no disputes because there was no enthusiasm. You can make pretty sure of peace if you will consent to put up with indifference. The hunting, smoking, drinking clergy of half a century ago 'cared for none of these things;' they rattled through their ten minutes' sermon once a week, visited a few of their wealthiest parishioners, occasionally read to a sick person if they were requested to do so, and considered their duty done. No one is so tolerant as a sceptic upon religious matters, simply because he does not concern himself in the least about them. You need fear no opposition from a dead body! Contention is at any rate a sign of life."

The elder clergyman sighed wearily.

"No doubt it is easy to be charitable and moderate when no deep feelings are involved in the discussion, but one *does* weary of all these disputes. Who, in my youth, would have believed that we should see clergymen actually going to law upon insignificant matters of ritual?"

"Nothing is insignificant that can be interpreted wrongly by the ignorant," broke in the younger man: "every minutiæ of the ritual that appears so unimportant in some eyes is intended to convey some secret meaning to the initiated. We do not object so much to the ritualistic ceremonial *in itself*, absurd and extravagant as it often is, but because it is the sign and symbol of various forms of the Romish persuasion."

"That may apply in some points, but surely not in all. I think much uncharitableness arises from very insignificant

causes. My neighbour in the next parish,
Mr. Ducie, is what some people call Ritualistic. Several of my brother clergy have
quarrelled with him on this account, but I
have attended his church once or twice,
and saw nothing that could justify me in
proceeding to that extremity. If he likes
to waste his parishioners' money and his
own, with burning wax candles on the
communion-table in broad daylight, that is
his affair entirely, and ought not to be
made a matter of dispute. Again, he wears
an extraordinary garment bordered with
gold, with a cross and a ship embroidered
on the back, and this is varied by a green
robe, worked all over with little crosses. I
think he makes himself look both undigni-
fied and absurd, and much more like a
Jewish priest than an English clergyman.
But, again, what is that to me? If he
became a heretic or an infidel, I should
withdraw myself from his society; but at
present I see no reason why he is not to be
treated as a Christian brother, more especially as he is one of the kindest and

most charitable of men. I believe fully, that as he is a very young man, these vagaries will pass away with the sober wisdom taught by maturer years. I am content to await that day in hope, and meantime am careful not to strengthen fanaticism by opposition. He shall not have the opportunity of considering himself a persecuted martyr as far as I am concerned."

"Sir, I assure you——" began the young curate eagerly, but he was interrupted by the announcement of luncheon, and soon after took his leave.

"Well, what do you think of him?" asked Mr. Helmore of his daughter, as the door closed behind the new arrival.

"I should think he was clever, papa, and certainly quite a gentleman, but he expresses his opinions with a good deal of freedom for so young a man."

"Ah! my dear, that is but natural; he is young and enthusiastic. These Oxford lights must think us steady-going old stagers terribly behind the times. I am glad he has come; he will wake us up a bit. One's ideas are apt to get rusty, living year after year in a retired place like this; sometimes one is almost tempted to regret."

"Regret what, dear papa?" asked Elizabeth, anxiously.

"Nothing, my child; nothing of any consequence. I have chosen my lot in life, and I must abide by it. Still I am glad Mr. Norman bids fair to be a profitable companion; one is never too old to learn, even from one's juniors."

Something in this remark touched Elizabeth; she laid her hand fondly on her father's arm, as she answered, with her eyes full of tears—

"You are the best, and kindest, and wisest father in the world, and Mr. Norman would do well if he were to learn from *you*. I do not like his domineering style of argument, and his remarks about the clergy of the last fifty years was almost rude, considering *your* age."

"Hush! my dear; he did not mean

that. I like the young man, and I am convinced [he will turn out a gem of a curate."

So the event proved. Elizabeth soon found she had very little time for sad and unprofitable musing, or for feeling her loneliness without Ida. Mr. Norman worked hard himself, and of course her assistance was required in everything. A new night-school was instituted—who could instruct the elder girls, but Elizabeth? An organ was placed in the church at the young curate's sole expense—and there was no one to play it but Elizabeth. A choir must be formed and instructed—and no lady would undertake the novel and arduous labour but Elizabeth. These and innumerable other duties fell to her share, and they were all cheerfully and readily undertaken.

Delighted at finding so untiring and energetic a prime minister, Mr. Norman dropped a little of his usual chilling reserve of manner to ladies, and condescended to talk to her of some of the schemes and projects that lay nearest his heart. Some of them appeared wild and Utopian enough to her calm, unromantic imagination, but she listened readily and kindly, and they became fast though most undemonstrative friends.

To a girl like Elizabeth it was really a satisfaction to have secured so able a help-mate for her father, without running the risk of any awkward situations for herself. Mr. Norman was so entirely wrapped up in his work, and besides this he was so tho-roughly a gentleman, and naturally so cold and reserved in manner, that his Rector's daughter could spend hours in his company without the least embarrassment or self-consciousness on either side.

Mr. Helmore was glad to see the friendly feeling that had sprung up between them, and by degrees almost resigned the reins of the spiritual government of the parish into their active and willing hands, secure that all would go well.

It was a strange, but not unprofitable, life for a young woman. By dint of living always with two most unworldly, though very talented, people, she lost any taint of fashionable young ladyism which might have lain dormant in her character. She became as active, as unwearied, as self-forgetting (a very different and a far harder thing than self-*denying*) as any young nun or hermit of the middle ages.

Mr. Helmore was amazed, Mr. Norman was delighted. Here was a brave disciple truly!—a lady, young and delicately nurtured, who would sit up all night beside a fever-stricken patient, with no more thought of infection or fatigue than one of the holy people of old mentioned above. No weather could deter her from her work, no task was too difficult or disagreeable for her to undertake.

Hitherto Mr. Norman had looked on all girls as a hindrance rather than a help in this work; a class useful and necessary in their way, no doubt, but, *as* a class, the reverse of congenial to him. But in Elizabeth Helmore he found none of the faults of her sex. She never expected any compliments, or anything beyond the most ordinary civility and attention ; she never required any coaxing to do her duty, and coquetry, impatience, and wilfulness seemed alike foreign to her nature.

"She is my right hand—she is simply *perfection !*" he exclaimed one day, in a fit of enthusiasm, to her father.

He smiled, and took the compliment at its proper worth, giving a loving, simple assent.

Truly, since those halcyon days when monks and nuns lived near together and even shared their holy work without thought of either love or wrangling, there has seldom existed a happier, more unworldly, more simple-minded party than these three at Arling Rectory.

Meanwhile the world looked on, wondered, and of course misunderstood.

"It is all coming right," wrote Mrs. Fletcher in a confidential letter to Ida. "Your father's new curate is everything he ought to be, and Elizabeth being of course everything *she* ought to be, there is no doubt that they will be married before the year is out. What a perfect couple they will be—they ought to reform the world!"

In consequence of this intimation, young Mrs. Atherstone wrote a letter to her sister, which provoked the following reply :—

"Dearest Ida,

"Mrs. Fletcher is (I *must* say it) a vulgar, gossiping woman. Mr. Norman has as little idea of marrying me as I have of marrying at all. We *are* a good deal together—it is necessary that it should be so—but do not credit any reports that may be spread to our disadvantage."

Ida showed these sentences to her husband, saying, with a smile—

"What can she mean, Arthur? '*To our disadvantage !'* One would think it was a sin to marry. I think it would be the best thing she could do."

"Elizabeth is growing romantic; that letter is not like her," was the answer.

"Depend upon it the new curate is trying
to teach her some of his new-fangled ideas,
and has partially succeeded."

Which was certainly true.

CHAPTER IX.

"If ladies be but young and fair,
They have the gift to know it."
SHAKESPEARE.

In one of the comfortable sitting-rooms of
the Bedford Hotel, Brighton, sits the young
bride, Ida Atherstone. Three weeks of
married life have altered her considerably.
She is handsomely dressed in dark green
velvet, with silver ornaments, a colour
admirably suited to her bright, pure complexion. The pretty golden hair is arranged
in a new and most becoming fashion, and
her attitude, as she leans back in the easy
chair, is quite perfect in its simple grace.
It is marvellous to note how soon the un-
tutored country girl has assumed the man-

10—2

ner and appearance of a grande dame, even
to the languid inflection of the voice, and
the easy dignity of each movement. Perhaps she overdoes it a *little*, but that will
soon wear off. Arthur considers her perfectly charming, and all Brighton is disposed to agree with him.

In that most delightful of autumn water-
ing places nice-looking girls, healthy-look-
ing girls, distinguished-looking girls, even
pretty girls, are common enough ; they
may be met with in crowds on the King's
Road, the Pier, or disporting themselves
gracefully at the Skating Rink, but nothing
so exquisitely and perfectly beautiful as
young Mrs. Atherstone had been seen there
of late years. The two infallible signs of a
beauty soon appeared ; the ladies all criti-
cised her, and the gentlemen were all dying
to be introduced to her.

Any young lady who is much " talked
about " by her own sex may be tolerably
certain that she is considered to be a
dangerous rival. Uninteresting, or plain
girls, can be safely left in peace to air their

innocuous attractions ; they need fear no enemies, and are allowed to pursue the even tenor of their ways in happy tranquillity. But envy, detraction, **and** even dislike are certain to follow in the steps of a girl who is either an acknowledged beauty, or possessed of that nameless, indefinable fascination which is, in reality, far more dangerous to the hearts of men.

Do you suppose the queen of beauties, that pearl among women, Mary Queen of Scots, owed her universal sway over the minds of all who beheld her, to her hazel eyes, her graceful figure, or her bands of glossy auburn hair ? Did Cleopatra govern Antony by her black eyes, her swarthy complexion, or her queenly presence ? No. Surely the influence of beauty may be great and all powerful for the time, but it is transient in its very nature. It was the bright witchery in the eyes of the Scottish queen, and her loving, yet coquettish ways that won all hearts, and all but subdued the sternest of the Calvinistic reformers so long as he was under the attraction of her immediate presence.

Had Cleopatra not been a genius as well as a woman, she had never so enchained her haughty warrior, and compelled him to forget alike his interests and his honour for the sake of her love.

To return from this digression. Ida Atherstone added to her beauty a wonderful charm and sweetness of manner, and it was *this*, even more than her personal attractions, which excited such universal admiration, and converted her young husband from a somewhat indifferent lover into her most devoted and submissive slave. Look at him now as he sits reading by the window, the light falls full on his face, and reveals clearly how bright and well he is looking. He seems ten years younger than when we saw him sitting alone in the Grange library, now more than two months ago. If any one had asked him the question, he would have stoutly affirmed that no man on earth ever was, or ever could be, so perfectly and intensely happy as himself.

It is nearly eleven o'clock, and Ida throws down her book.

"Arthur, don't you think we ought to go out? It is such a glorious morning."

"To be sure; I had forgotten the time. Get your things on, darling, I am quite ready."

In five minutes they are out on the sunny Parade, already crowded with people, early as it is.

"Let us go to the Rink," says Arthur; "there is no wind; it is just the morning for you to learn to skate."

"I shall only tumble down, and make myself a ridiculous spectacle," she laughs.

"Never mind, every one tumbles down. I believe it is quite the exception for any one to keep upright. Hullo! who's that?"

This exclamation was occasioned by the sight of two young ladies, who were walking on in front. I said two *young* ladies, but on a nearer inspection it is evident that one of them must have numbered at least five and thirty summers, in spite of her unexceptionable figure and youthfully-

arranged flaxen locks. She had apparently
heard Captain Atherstone's exclamation, for
she instantly looked round, and in another
minute they were cordially shaking hands,
and Ida was introduced to Lady Laura
Marjoribanks and her daughter Alda.

The young lady was about Ida's own
age, perhaps a year or two younger, and
appeared painfully shy, colouring up to her
ears when she was addressed, and apparently desiring nothing so much as to
remain entirely unnoticed. Arthur walked
on with her, endeavouring to make her
enter into conversation in his kind, cordial
way, and the two married ladies fell behind
together.

With one glance of her keen, light eyes,
Lady Laura had seen that her companion
was young, beautiful, and elegantly dressed,
and she *knew* her to be wealthy and well
connected—at any rate, through her husband's family. She was, therefore, in every
sense, well worth cultivating, and it was in
an unusually cordial tone of voice that her
adyship commenced the conversation.

"What a charming place this is in autumn, Mrs. Atherstone! I always say that Brighton is the only town I ever visited in November in which one hears people complain of having too much sunshine."

"It seems very pleasant," replied Ida, a scarcely perceptible shade of diffidence in her tone. It was the first time in her life that she had ever spoken to a real live ladyship, and she felt uncertain as to whether she should use her title or not.

"Of course you know it well," continued Lady Laura. "You have always lived in Sussex, have you not?"

"Yes, but we never came to Brighton; indeed, we never went anywhere. I have only seen London once, about seven years ago, when papa took me up to see a dentist."

Lady Laura opened her eyes. Here was a novice, indeed, in the fashionable world. Here, surely, was an opportunity for her universal benevolence to exercise itself. For Lady Laura *was* a very benevolent person—at least she considered herself so.   There was nothing that gave her greater pleasure than to take some débutante by the hand, be she married or single —in the first instance with the object of obtaining for them a favourable reception into the most exclusive clique in the world, the crême de la crême of London society —in the latter, to procure them introductions and opportunities which should result in a grand matrimonial triumph in St. George's or Westminster Abbey.

Hitherto her efforts had not always been attended with success, but she was by no means discouraged, and hailed a new and promising pupil with as much joy as Frederick the Great did an unusually tall recruit to swell the magnificence of his guard of honour.   So her ladyship instantly formed the resolution to " take up " Ida, and give her some notion of the fashionable world that was so new to her, and in which she was so well fitted to shine.   It was therefore in a tone of increased friendliness that she continued the conversation.

" This gay scene must be new to you,

then, Mrs. Atherstone. Arling is quite a retired little village, is it not ?"

" How in the world did she know I came from Arling ?" thought Ida ; but she answered simply in the affirmative.

" Not much conversation," thought Lady Laura. " Poor young thing ! she is very shy. I must try and draw her out."

"I am so glad to have this unexpected opportunity of making your acquaintance," she said, taking the young wife's arm in hers, with a sudden accession of cordiality, at which Ida did not know whether to be most frightened or pleased. " I have been intimate with your husband's family for so many years, and it gratifies one of the dearest wishes of my heart to see Arthur so happily married."

Ida blushed, looked down, and began to think her new acquaintance a very fascinating person.

" I shall hope to see a great deal of you while we are here, dear Mrs. Atherstone ; we have taken a house in Palmeira Square for two months—I suppose you will not be here so long ?"

"Oh! no; I believe Arthur means us to go on to Torquay next week. I have not seen Lady Atherstone yet—since my marriage, I mean."

"Ah! but he must not hurry you off so soon as that; there are some capital balls coming on in a few days. Mrs. Archibald Douglas gives one on the 29th. You do not know her, I suppose?"

"No; I know no one here."

"Ah! perhaps that is just as well; a very young married lady like you cannot be too careful of her acquaintances in a place like Brighton. There is an enormous mixture here, and, I am sorry to say, very few unexceptionable people. Ah! here we are at the Rink—what a pretty sight it is!"

Certainly it *was* a pretty sight, and to Ida's unaccustomed eyes it appeared quite charming. She did not trouble her head as to whether all the performers were "unexceptionable" people or not; they were most of them young and well dressed, and many of them remarkably nice-looking. Some were skimming along with the easy grace of birds on the wing, some were advancing cautiously with the aid of a stick or some friendly arm, and some dashed into the conflict with a dangerous bravery, which usually ended in an ignominious downfall about every five minutes.

" How *delightful* it looks, Arthur ; do let me try," exclaimed Ida, quite forgetful of her previous fears.

Miss Marjoribanks was equally anxious to make the attempt, and in a few minutes both young ladies were standing on the asphalte, while Lady Laura cackled on the edge, like a careful mother hen who beholds her adventurous brood attempting to cross the water.

" Now take care, Alda, my dear ; you will be over. My dear Mrs. Atherstone, don't attempt to move alone. Good gracious ! there's another one down ! My dear Arthur, *do* tell them to come off, it is *really* a most dangerous amusement !"

The effect of all these exclamations **was** to make her daughter so painfully nervous, that she found it wholly impossible to advance a step; but Ida only laughed and struck out boldly, disdaining even her husband's assistance.

As a general rule, a salmon on a gravel path is in a happy and appropriate situation compared with a young lady who is attempting roller-skating for the first time, but Arthur always said that it was impossible for Ida to appear awkward in any situation, however trying or ludicrous to less graceful people, and his words were fully borne out on the present occasion. While other beginners were floundering and rolling about in every direction, she went on her way, slowly, indeed, and diffidently, but with a certain ease, composure, and, above all, safety, which excited much envy and admiration.

"What a lovely girl!" remarked a young officer, as she passed; "who is she?"

"I have not the least idea," replied his companion; "she is certainly pretty, but shocking bad style. You see she is all alone; and that bright golden hair is always dyed."

Ida caught the remark, and the idea

seemed to her so supremely ridiculous that she burst out laughing, thereby seriously endangering her balance. Indeed, she must have fallen, but a strong arm caught her, to which she clung nervously for a moment, without seeing to whom she was indebted for the timely assistance.

When she looked up she saw a pair of bright dark eyes, regarding her with considerable surprise and attention, and their owner, who was no other than Lord Trevor, exclaimed, with some embarrassment—

"Mrs. Atherstone, I believe? You must allow me to introduce myself. Perhaps you may have heard your husband speak of Launcelot Trevor."

"Certainly I have," she replied with animation. "You are *great* friends, are you not?"

"I hope I may call myself so. Here is Arthur himself. My good fellow, allow me to congratulate you. Your wife has had a narrow escape of a broken arm."

"If it had not been for your kind intervention," the young wife added, laughing, as she quitted Lord Trevor's arm for her husband's.

"My dear Trevor, is it really you?" exclaimed Arthur in much astonishment. "I had no idea that we should see you here."

"Neither had I the slightest expectation of meeting you," replied his friend. "Now that we are aware of each other's proximity, I shall do myself the honour of calling. You are at the Grand, of course."

"No—at the Bedford. Come in to tea this afternoon, will you?"

"With the greatest pleasure. Arthur, who *is* that frantic woman standing on the edge of the Rink? She will be over in a minute. I declare she is making signals to you."

"No doubt," replied Arthur, laughing. "It is Lady Laura Marjoribanks; she came here with us, and has been in an agony of fright ever since. We can't be bothered with answering her signals now. If she glances this way she will have the satisfaction of seeing that we are yet alive. Come, Ida, are you rested?"

They moved on, and Lord Trevor, raising his hat, skated away with easy grace, and was soon lost to sight in the crowd.

By the time the Atherstones had navigated their way to Lady Laura, they found her just ready for departure, having captured her daughter, whose performance on the skates had been of a very limited character. She took leave of our young couple with much affection, promising to call in a day or two.

Ida remained for an hour or so, and by the time she left the Rink was qualified to consider herself a very fair performer.

"What a pleasant man Lord Trevor seems to be!" she remarked to her husband that afternoon, as they were sitting in their cosy sitting-room, over the walnuts and wine which followed their early dinner.

"He is a *very* good fellow," was the hearty answer; "eccentric in some things, but the best-hearted man in the world."

"Why is he not married? He looks older than you."

"He is, some years older; but that is one of his oddities. He is capable of admiring a pretty girl, no man more so, but he always says he never intends to trust his honour and his happiness in any woman's hands. For all his gay, jolly manner, he has the most deeply-rooted prejudices of any man I ever knew. He has but a poor opinion of the sex, foolish fellow."

"Perhaps he has been jilted."

"Oh, no! he would have told me if any thing of that kind had taken place. So far from that, he has never even had so much as a flirtation with any woman, married or unmarried."

Ida rose and walked to the window, as if somewhat weary of the subject, but nevertheless her mind was running on what she had heard.

"I could fancy," she thought to herself, "I could fancy, if one was disengaged, that it would be a very exciting pursuit to try and subjugate a man like Lord Trevor. It is strange that a young nobleman, so handsome and wealthy as he is, should be so determined a misogynist. It is not natural —there must be some history about him. I will ask Lady Laura."

"Oh, Arthur!" Captain Atherstone had risen from the table and walked to his wife's side, passing his hand affectionately round her waist. She moved a little uneasily. "Take care, Arthur; don't do that, please; we are rather *en évidence* from this window."

"It is all right, dear; no one can see me. Come here; I want you to look at this ring."

She turned round, and he took an opal ring from his pocket, and slipped it on one of her delicate little fingers.

"Oh, how lovely! where did it come from?"

"It was my mother's; she gave it to me for you, but I have always forgotten about it. It is an old family ring, Ida, so you must take care of it. There is a tradition that great misfortune will befall our house if it is ever lost or given away."

"Of course I will take care of it, dear

11—2

Arthur. How good of you to let me wear it !"

He bent to kiss her, and at that moment the door opened, and the servant announced Lord Trevor. He followed so quickly, that the married lovers had barely time to separate.

Ida came forward with blushing cheeks, and in her haste the precious ring fell to the ground from her hand, and Lord Trevor trod it under foot.

He restored it uninjured, with many apologies, and Ida smiled her forgiveness; but, strange to say, Arthur, usually so ready to overlook any little accident, appeared somewhat annoyed.

"It is a valuable ring, Ida," he said; " you should not be so careless with it."

She made no profession of sorrow, but pouted her pretty scarlet lips—a proceeding which ruins most women's beauty, but only served to enhance hers. So, at least, thought Lord Trevor, though the reverse might have been inferred from his manner.

He turned to Arthur, and began an

animated conversation with him, which lasted for nearly an hour, scarcely interchanging a word with the young wife, who sat silent, but observing.

When at last he took his leave, Arthur turned to her, saying, with a smile—

"Well, was not I right about him, dear? Is he not the only man in England who would have sat an hour in the presence of a girl like *you*, and scarcely make a remark to her?"

"Wait a little," she replied; "he will like me better by-and-by."

CHAPTER X.

" Heaven from all creatures hides the book of fate."
                                                    POPE.

NEXT day, about three o'clock, young Mrs.
Atherstone was lying on the sofa in their sitting-room, absorbed in the exciting pages of
one of Miss Braddon's novels. Any species of
sensational reading was entirely new to her,
and it is not too much to say that her present freedom of choice in this respect was
regarded by her as one of the peculiar advantages of married life. It may be that
Arthur should have prevented this, or, at
any rate, tried to divert the current of her
mind into a more improving channel, but,
to say the truth, it did not occur to him.
So she read with avidity everything that

was sent her from the library, good, bad, and indifferent ; and when conscience pricked her as to the waste of time involved, and the utter uselessness of such employment, she would endeavour to convince herself that she was gaining much knowledge of the world which was unknown to her before, and which was indispensable to a young married lady in her position.

It was true that she was gaining much knowledge of the world, but it was a knowledge that had better have been kept from her. The unnatural crimes and dark intrigues which form the plots of so many of our modern stories, are, in truth, intensely interesting, and often exciting, but the morbid character of such feelings is sufficiently shown by the distaste engendered in habitual novel readers to every kind of improving and innocent literature. It seems as " dull, flat, and unprofitable " to them as bread and milk to a child whose appetite has been vitiated by curries and sweetmeats. It may be questioned whether

sensational' novels are of real use to any
class of society except the over-worked
man of business, whose mind needs and
hails the excitement of such reading after
a long day's hard mental labour as an abso-
lute rest and refreshment.

The same argument may apply to many
of our modern amusements, but Ida had no
such excuse.   Yet look at her now, as she
leans back on the soft pillows, her blue
eyes bent with eager interest on the page
before her, her fair cheeks flushed with the
exciting climax, which is invariably reached
at the end of the second volume.   Arthur
has gone out for a stroll on the Parade,
tired of waiting, and Ida has no distrac-
tion to draw her attention from her book.
Indeed, so absorbed is she, that a thundering knock falls unheeded on her ear, and
the door opens, and Lady Laura Marjoribanks is announced, before she can recall
her ideas to the events of ordinary life.

"I am so glad to find you in, dear Mrs.
Atherstone," says her ladyship, advancing
with outstretched hand.   "I caught sight

of Arthur alone on the Parade, so I judged
that you were at home, most likely pre-
paring to join him. Is it so? Shall I in-
terfere with your walk?"

"Indeed, no, Lady Laura. I did not
mean to go out for an hour, at any rate."

"Ah, I am glad of that, for I wanted to
have a long comfortable chat with you.
Alda is on the cliff with my friend, Mrs.
Douglas, and I told her to come here in
half an hour's time."

"I wish you had brought her."

"Oh, she is very happy, looking at the
shops. Mrs. Douglas is very kind to her;
she is one of the few people who appreciate
my poor girl, and she *is* a good girl, in spite
of her unfortunate looks."

"Unfortunate looks!" exclaimed Ida, in
astonishment. "What is there unfortunate
in her looks, Lady Laura?"

"Oh, my dear Mrs. Atherstone, surely
you need not ask; hers is the most *hopeless* style of ugliness. That miserable flaxen
hair, which looks as if it ought to be golden,
and some wicked fairy had rubbed all the

gold off. And those small, pale, pinched-up features, with that wretchedly unhappy expression, as if some one was perpetually pinching her. And then, poor girl, her figure! I go to the best dress-makers, but what can they do with such irremediably high shoulders, and such a fatally thick waist as Alda's. I assure you my waistbands will not meet round her by a good inch and a half. It is perfectly awful, and at seventeen! What will she be at seven and twenty? I shudder to think of it."

"She seems most amiable and good," observed Ida, scarcely knowing what to reply.

"Ah, well, she *is* that, I must say. But, after all, I suppose, most young ladies are good, and as for amiability, it is a very negative sort of recommendation. I never was the least amiable myself, and I have done very well in the world. Now let us talk about yourself, dear Mrs. Atherstone. By the bye, I wish you would let me call you Ida. It seems strange to ask it after so short an acquaintance, but I know all your dear husband's family so intimately, and——"

" Please do, Lady Laura, I should like it so much better. I am not yet used to my married name. Arthur is quite amused by the way I stare at him sometimes when he introduces me as Mrs. Atherstone."

" Ah, that is very natural. I remember feeling the same just after I was married. To be sure, I married very young; I was two months younger than my daughter is now."

" Only seventeen ?"

" Only just seventeen, and poor Sir Leonard was nearly thirty years older. He has been dead eleven years now. I will tell you all about my married life some day, it will amuse you ; but now I want to talk about yourself. I have an invitation here for you to Mrs. Archibald Douglas's ball on Thursday. You will like to go, will you not ?"

" It is very kind of you, Lady Laura, but—I scarcely know. I have never been

to a ball in my life, and I have not a ball-
dress in the world."

"Oh, that is of no consequence. Han-
nington's people will make you up a nice
dress in a few days. We can go and see
about it this afternoon. You have no en-
gagements?"

"Oh, no; but there is one thing I am
not *quite* sure if Arthur would like me to
think of going to a ball just now while his
sister is so ill. I should scarcely like to
propose it."

"Oh, that is nonsense, my dear; she
may go on in the same state for months.
He can't expect you to shut yourself up on
account of a sister-in-law whom you have
never seen. I think better of Arthur than
to suppose he can be so unreasonable. Ah,
here is Alda," as that young lady was
announced. "Come in, my dear child,.
and don't look as if you were being con-
ducted to execution. You know Mrs.
Atherstone."

Ida shook hands kindly with the poor
girl, who blushed up to the eyes at her

mother's remark, and Lady Laura took
her leave, after making an arrangement to
meet at the corner of East Street in half
an hour's time, in order that they might go
together to choose the ball-dress.

When they had gone Ida went up to
dress, feeling a little dissatisfied. "I am
horribly weak," she thought to herself; "I
know I ought not to have given way about
that ball. I am afraid Arthur will be
annoyed, but fortunately there is still time
to ask him about it." She hurried on her
hat and jacket, and went downstairs, but,
alas! when she reached the Parade, no
Arthur was to be seen. He had probably
got tired of waiting, and gone to the read-
ing-room, or perhaps to the Rink. She stood
irresolute for a moment, feeling considerably annoyed at her position, for to this
country girl the mere fact of being alone
amongst a crowd, many of whom stared at
her with evident admiration, was embar-
rassing in the extreme. She began to consider whether it would not be best to leave
Lady Laura in the lurch, and beat a retreat

to the hotel, when she heard herself addressed, and turning hastily, she saw Lord Trevor.

"You seem to be looking for some one, Mrs. Atherstone; can I be of any assistance?"

"Oh, thank you, so much; I don't quite know what to do. I can't see Arthur anywhere, and I am quite alone, and—and—the people *do* stare so." She was very near tears.

He smiled. "Will you take my arm? We will see if we cannot find Arthur. He is not far off, for I saw him five minutes ago."

Accordingly, they walked together down the Parade; but among the many young men answering to the same description— "tall, fair, with a low black hat and grey coat"—no Arthur was to be seen.

"I wonder you do not drive here, Mrs. Atherstone," remarked his lordship, thinking it best to try and make some conversation. "I know you *can* drive very well, for I have seen you."

"Where? Oh, no, you cannot!——"

" Indeed I have ; I was with Mrs. Fletcher that morning when you drove into Daylesford alone on a market-day, and got rather into difficulties in a crowded street. You must remember it, it is not so very long ago."

" Oh, yes, how strange that you should have been there ! I never saw you."

" No, but I saw *you*, and from something I heard in the town that day, I imagined that you would shortly be married to Arthur. I taxed him with it the next day, but he denied it most emphatically— the sly fellow."

" Did he ?"

" He did, indeed. I hope you have cured him of telling stories, Mrs. Atherstone."

So, talking merrily, they paced up and down, till Ida uttered an exclamation of joy.

" There is Arthur. Thank you so much, Lord Trevor. I do not know what I should have done without you."

He raised his hat, and turned back, while she joined her husband.

"My dear Ida," he exclaimed, "have you been alone ?"

"No, indeed; Lord Trevor has been taking charge of me. I could not imagine what had become of you; we had been walking up and down for nearly half an hour."

"That was good natured of Trevor; as a rule, he hates walking with a lady. My dear child, how you are racing !"

"Yes, we must make haste; I promised Lady Laura to meet her in East Street, and she must be waiting."

As they walked quickly along, she told Arthur about the ball at Mrs. Douglas's, and Lady Laura's offer of superintending her costume.

"You don't mind, Arthur, do you ?" she said, glancing up earnestly in his face. "Tell me if you do."

"No, dear; not if you really wish to go."

An affectionate wife would surely have noted the hesitating tone, and inquired the reason; but Ida was quite satisfied, and thought she had fully discharged her duty.

"It is very kind of Lady Laura," she said; "I can't think what should make her take such an interest in me."

"She is rather fond of taking up young married people. I do not want you to become *very* intimate, Ida, dear, she is not quite the best style of person. My mother dislikes her very much."

"Arthur, what *do* you mean? Surely her style must be unexceptionable; she is an earl's daughter."

"There are some duchesses whom I should be sorry to see you resemble. Your father has taught you the good old Conservative reverence for rank, but it is very far from being an infallible test of worth in society."

",I suppose not. But you would not call Lady Laura unladylike."

"That is not quite what I mean. Ah! there she is. I will go on to the library, Ida. No doubt Lady Laura will see you home."

He turned away, and Ida joined her friends, and in ten minutes' time had

completely forgotten the slight sense of uneasiness caused by her husband's words in
the excitement of choosing a regular ball-
room outfit under the superintendence of
Lady Laura.

Meanwhile Lord Trevor was walking
along the cliff in solitary meditation, when
he was hailed by a loud voice.

" Hollo, Trevor, where are you off to ?"

" Hollo, Moncrieff, who thought of seeing
you down here ?"

" I am glad to see you, old fellow; I
have not met a soul I know yet, and I have
been here three days.   There's nothing so
disgusting as being alone in a crowd."

" Very true.   Come along, and let us have
a look at the young ladies.   Did you ever see
such costumes ?   Look at that girl in front :
she is a regular aviary—a bird in her hat,
a bird in her muff, a bird at her throat, and
a couple of birds swinging from her ears."

" Absurd, is it not ?   By the bye, did I
see you just now walking with Atherstone's
pretty wife ?"

" Yes ; do you know her ?"

"No; but I saw them at Folkestone. What an exquisite face she has! You seemed on excellent terms, Trevor, eh?"

"She is very pretty, but she has not much to say—quite a little country girl."

"Ah! I forgot. To be sure Atherstone is a bosom friend of yours, so no doubt you would consider it beneath you to venture on the smallest flirtation."

"Certainly I should; but fortunately there is no temptation—I am not the least attracted by her."

(Oh! Lord Trevor, is that *quite* true?)

"Well, I am not bound in that way," replied Captain Moncrieff, "and I must say I should like to have another look at those blue eyes."

"Ah! that is all you fellows think of. For my part, I can't imagine what induced Arthur to marry a mere pretty doll like that. He is the best fellow in the world: I do not believe the woman exists who is really worthy of him."

"No doubt you think so. Well, I must

be off, Trevor. Look me up at the Bedford some day, will you ?"

He strolled away, and Lord Trevor, meeting Arthur soon after, walked up and down with him till the shades of evening began to descend, and the Parade was wholly deserted.

CHAPTER XI.

" My good blade carves the casques of men,
    My tough lance thrusteth sore,
My strength is as the strength of ten,
    Because my heart is pure."

TENNYSON.

" IT would be the greatest possible help,
Miss Helmore ; but of course you must not
overtire yourself."

" Indeed, Mr. Norman, I do not feel the
least overworked. I am sorry you had
the trouble of coming here so early. Your
time is valuable, and a message sent by one
of the school-children would have done
quite well."

Elizabeth was sitting in the Rectory
drawing-room as she spoke, and opposite
her stood the curate, of course bent as

usual on some eager and immediate reform. She was looking very nice this morning, dressed in a dove-coloured merino, a bow of blue ribbon at the neck—her favourite colour—and with no other sort of ornament except her watch-chain. Her smooth, fair cheeks were unusually blooming, and there was the light of a steadfast purpose in her blue eyes. But had she resembled Lot's wife after her transformation into the salt pillar, Mr. Norman could not have regarded her (or perhaps I should say her outward appearance) with more complete indifference. He was wholly bent on the object in view, which was certainly an important one.

"I think my plan good," he continued. "I wanted to talk it over with you, so I could not send a messenger. It seems to me that a Bible-class, held here by you once a week, expressly for young girls between the ages of fifteen and twenty, would be a very useful and valuable undertaking. This parish is so large and so outlying, that the difficulty of getting any hold on the young women is enormous. I have absolutely not an evening free during the week, or I would not have troubled you."

"Indeed I shall be glad to do it, Mr. Norman; at any rate I will try, though I have had very little experience of that kind of teaching—with young women, I mean."

"You may encounter a few obstacles at first, but they will disappear before your energy and perseverance. I do not know another young lady of your age who could wisely begin such an undertaking, but your capabilities are great. You are blest with so much good temper and clear practical sense, that you might safely enter on any work of this kind. I wish I could say as much of any other lady in the neighbourhood."

"The Miss Ducies are anxious for some work; their own parish is so very small. Do you not think they might be asked to assist in some way?"

"Heaven forbid!" exclaimed the young curate; "their presence would be sufficient to breed discord and schism in the parish.

The youngest has much zeal, but it is
wholly untempered with discretion, and the
eldest is a rank Puseyite—in other words,
a moderate Roman Catholic."

Elizabeth inherited too much of her
father's gentle, tolerant nature to join in
this very sweeping condemnation, and she
replied gently—

"Marion Ducie is much beloved in their
own parish. I believe hers is a most unselfish life."

"Very possibly; but nevertheless some
of her proceedings are only to be explained
by the supposition that she is a little de-
ranged. I am told that she has adopted
the American notion that popular tunes are
the most suitable for sacred poetry, and
that she insists on her school-children
shouting out the 'Marseillaise' to holy
words, and one of our most beautiful hymns
is degraded by being sung to the air of
'Drink to me only with thine eyes.'"*

"It is certainly injudicious," answered

* This last is a fact.

Elizabeth, with a smile, "but they mean no harm, and it may not strike the poor people as anything irreverent."

"Perhaps not; but I should object to that sort of thing here. Miss Helmore, would you kindly let me glance at your Coal and Provident Society accounts? I find mine are not quite correct."

In a moment both the dark heads were bent over Elizabeth's neat columns of figures; and neither caught sight of a lady who walked briskly up the gravel path, and, being evidently on familiar terms with the family, just glanced in at the window, and then entered the house without the ceremony of knocking. It was Mrs. Fletcher, looking considerably heated and discomposed. Her heavy velvet bonnet was pushed back from her flushed brow, and her hands quite trembled with excitement as she knocked at Mr. Helmore's study door.

A gentle "Come in," replied, and the good lady entered, and straightway sank into the chair that was courteously offered her.

She was decidedly in an excited and per-
turbed frame of mind, but the sight of the
venerable old man, with his snowy head and
unruffled brow, had the effect of calming
her very considerably.   There was something in the influence of Mr. Helmore's
presence, and the glance of his kind, yet
keen, blue eyes, which had a wonderful
effect on her coarser nature ; and when, at
last, she found breath to speak, her tone
was gentle, and even a little embarrassed,
though her words were somewhat abrupt.

"Mr. Helmore, I have called to speak to
you about your daughter."

"About Ida ?"

"No ; about Elizabeth."

"Indeed !"

Mr. Helmore paused, much surprised.

Mrs. Fletcher bent forward, and spoke
earnestly and emphatically, but still with
moderation.

"Mr. Helmore, you will excuse my
speaking very plainly.   I have known your
two dear girls since they were born, and I
think, next to yourself, no one can take

more interest in them than I do. I had no hand in Ida's marriage; even the probability of such an event was concealed from me till the last moment; but I am resolved not to be hoodwinked *this* time. Things are not going on as they should, Mr. Helmore; believe me, things are not going on as they should."

"Indeed, Mrs. Fletcher, I am at a loss to understand what you can mean," was the bewildered yet dignified reply. "My eldest daughter, at any rate, is not likely to have committed any imprudence. I would as soon suspect myself as her."

"My dear sir, Elizabeth is an angel, but she is more fitted to be the abbess of a Carmelite convent than a young lady of the nineteenth century. In many things she has clear, practical common sense (more than most people), but in matters relating to the proprieties she is as ignorant and as innocent as a new-born baby."

Matters relating to the proprieties! Mr. Helmore grew more and more puzzled.

"I should be obliged to you, Mrs.

Fletcher, if you would explain yourself
clearly," he said at last.

Mrs. Fletcher rose from her seat and
assumed an attitude absolutely tragic, while
her voice almost shook with suppressed
feeling.

" I *will* speak plainly, Mr. Helmore, and
to do so, I will ask your attention for only
a very few minutes. I allude to your
eldest daughter's intimacy with your
curate, Mr. Norman; I allude to the long
walks they constantly take together in
daylight and in dusk, to the private inter-
views which take place daily between
them, to the notes which are continually
interchanged; in a word, to the whole of
the unaccountable and most imprudent
intercourse which has become the common
talk of the neighbourhood, and bids fair to
destroy your daughter's peace of mind for
ever. If the young man's intentions are
open and honourable, let him declare his
attachment, if——"

Mr. Helmore had hitherto listened with
a sort of stunned feeling, composed partly

of surprise and horror, but perhaps chiefly of very genuine indignation. But now he deemed it well to interrupt the voluble lady, and he did so decisively, but still calmly.

"You are mistaken, Mrs. Fletcher, and I must request that you will not continue to speak in this way. I have the fullest confidence in Elizabeth's good sense and discretion, and I have also a very high opinion of my curate. They are unavoidably thrown much together, as my daughter takes so active a part in parish matters, but there has been nothing like imprudence."

"Ah, you do not know."

"Pardon me, I am acquainted with all my daughter's movements—as a rule I know where she is every hour of the day. As for the evening walks to which you allude, I conclude that she has been sometimes joined by Mr. Norman on her way back from the night school. It was considerate of him if it was so, and I am much obliged to him for it. I have been some-

times a little uneasy at her coming home
alone these dark evenings."

Mrs. Fletcher elevated her eyes and
hands.

"And I am to conclude then that you
approve of all this intimate intercourse
between Elizabeth and a young man you
have scarcely known five weeks."

"I see no reason to disapprove of it; I
have perfect confidence in them both."

"You see of course the natural sequel
to all this—they will be married before
the year is out."

An annoyed flush rose to Mr. Helmore's
brow.

"I do not think so," he replied; "I do
not anticipate anything of the kind; in fact,
I may affirm positively that such a union
never will take place. Mr. Norman does
not approve of the clergy marrying——"

"Then Mr. Norman must be a snake in
the grass, or a fool," broke from Mrs.
Fletcher's impatient lips.

There was no reply.

"Well, I have no more to say," said the

good lady at last, rising, " if you see no reason for interfering, of course it is not my business to say another word. I suppose you would not approve of my giving a hint to Elizabeth ?"

" Indeed, I think it would be better not. Good-bye, Mrs. Fletcher, I am sure you meant kindly by coming to me this morning ; you must forgive me for not taking your advice."

In another moment she was walking down the gravel path, feeling considerably snubbed and depressed. In her own circle, at Daylesford, she was an oracle, partly owing to the superior position she occupied in the little country town, and partly to her peculiarly positive, dictatorial style of talking, which passed for wisdom with many people. Yet she felt she had made no impression on this gentle, unworldly, old-fashioned country clergyman ; on the contrary, she had been made to feel very small in her own estimation, and almost as if she had been impertinently intrusive in offering her advice.

Under these humiliating circumstances, it was a real gratification at this moment to behold the young curate himself, walking down the turnpike-road a little in front. It was true that Mr. Norman's pace was extremely fast, even for a young man, and Mrs. Fletcher was stout, and a good deal heated, but the opportunity was too good to be lost. So she toiled and panted along the hard road, till within speaking distance, when she raised a feeble call, which fortunately succeeded in rousing the Curate's attention.

He turned at once, and beholding his fair pursuer, flushed and exhausted, he kindly offered his arm. She could not refuse, for she felt really tired, but it was not quite what she had intended. It is difficult to put a series of searching questions to a young man, and perhaps finish by giving him a severe lecture, while all the time you are clinging fast to his arm for support.

But her undaunted spirit rose the higher for this apparent obstacle, and after a few preliminary observations on the weather &c., she dashed into the subject with somewhat injudicious haste.

"Elizabeth Helmore is a remarkably nice girl, Mr. Norman."

"She is indeed," he replied warmly, "she is the greatest help to me in the parish, I cannot think how we should get on without her."

Come, this is encouraging, thought his interlocutor, and her next question went some degrees nearer the mark.

"She would make an excellent wife, Mr. Norman."

"Yes, happy the man who wins her. I never met her equal among young ladies, such clear common sense and absence of affectation."

"Very true, and such a sweet temper."

"Such indefatigable industry."

"Such an affectionate heart."

"So thoroughly orthodox in her views."

"So *very* unselfish."

"With such a talent for teaching."

"I do believe he is going to confide in

me," thought the delighted lady, hanging with increased warmth of affection on the curate's arm. "I will give him an opening."

"Mr. Helmore would be pleased to see Elizabeth comfortably married."

"Do you think so?"

"Indeed I do, especially to a clergyman."

"Really? I should have thought her marriage the greatest misfortune that could happen to him. They are so devoted to each other."

"Ah, that is true, but he is an unselfish father, and would rejoice in his daughter's happiness. No, Mr. Norman, he would oppose no such short-sighted objections to your—to her wishes."

"Ah, well, you know him best. Do you see we are building a new room for the infants on to the school, Mrs. Fletcher? Will it not be an improvement?"

"Yes, yes, no doubt, but to return to the subject we were discussing, I think that as a clergyman's wife——"

"Pray excuse my interrupting you, Mrs. Fletcher. I see our schoolmaster in front; I must try and catch him. I have an important message to deliver."

"To be sure. But, talking of Elizabeth, don't you agree with me that, as a clergyman's wife, she would shine a bright example to this parish, or to any parish?"

"No doubt she would. My *own* opinion is entirely adverse to the marriage of the clergy; but that would not, of course, affect Miss Helmore's views. I *must hasten* on, Mrs. Fletcher. Excuse me. Good morning."

And he was off, striding along the hard road, as if (to use an expression of Mrs. Fletcher's when narrating the whole scene at home) he "had the seven-leagued boots on."

Foiled on every point, she descended the steep road into the village, where her carriage was waiting.

"After all, I have done no good," she thought; "and I fear I have only put the young man on his guard. What a very

13---2

disappointing conversation, to be sure ! I
thought we were getting on so nicely. I
do hope he won't go and repeat anything I
have said."

She need not have troubled herself; Mr.
Norman straightway forgot the entire conversation; and if ever it reverted to his
mind, it was only in the form of a sincere
wish that no human being, layman or clergyman, would ever make an offer of marriage to Miss Helmore; for if by any unlucky chance she accepted it, what would
become of the night-school ?

So the little party at Arling went on
their way in peace. Even Mr. Helmore
soon dismissed the disagreeable impression
which had been left on his mind by Mrs.
Fletcher's warning, and smiled to himself
as he looked at Elizabeth's calm, unruffled
face, and Mr. Norman's enthusiastic absorp-
tion in his work. Ida's letters dropped in
occasionally, almost like missives from another planet, so different was the atmosphere of worldliness, excitement, and
pleasure which they breathed, to the tran-

quil, intensely practical life led at the Rectory. Sometimes when she received one of these daintily-scented notes, with their elaborate blue-and-gold monogram, Elizabeth would hold it dreamily unopened in her hand, and muse how it would have been if Ida had not married, or——if *she* had been the one chosen by Arthur. She would chide herself afterwards for indulging in such vain and unprofitable thoughts, but nevertheless they were her real safeguard against any possible danger which might have arisen from her intercourse with Mr. Norman.

Oh, Arthur! blind, honourable, devoted, mistaken husband! had you but waited and observed a *little* longer—had you not gone to work in such haste to repair an imaginary wrong, you might have gained a heart noble and pure indeed—a heart which would have remained yours in all faithfulness till it ceased to beat!

Sweet Elizabeth Helmore! it was well for her that the regular, steady, practical business of life prevented that half-conscious

feeling from developing into a heart-ache.
The calm sweetness of her nature was still
unembittered by any real regrets.   But
nevertheless this was the reason that so
early in life she began to lead the life of
a Protestant nun, caring only for her father
and her sister, and never even casting a wish
towards the happy married life which is the
desired bourne of most girls.   I do not
think she was the less bright and contented
for this.

In our state of society marriage certainly
occupies a far too prominent place in the
minds of our young women.   If the right man
comes accept him by all means, gratefully
and rejoicingly, but if not—do not marry for
the mere sake of being married, or sink
into a state of listless apathy and despair.
We have the highest authority for saying
that though a man who gives a daughter in
marriage does " well," he who keeps her at
home does " better."

" Old maids " are the kindest race in the
world, the most unselfish, the most useful.
Cheer up, my unmarried sister of five-and-

thirty or forty : yours, after all, is the most peaceful lot in this life, and assuredly it will not be the least blessed in the next !

CHAPTER XII.

"Then Arthur charged his warrior whom he loved
And honoured most, Sir Launcelot, to ride forth
And bring the Queen."

TENNYSON.

"Look here, Launcelot, what on earth am I to do?" The speaker was Captain Atherstone, and he was addressing Lord Trevor as they stood together in the coffee-room of the Bedford Hotel. "I have just received this letter from my mother, and I don't see how I can delay an hour. Yet I can't bear to disappoint Ida; the poor child is upstairs at this moment trying on her dress."

His friend took the note held out to him, and read as follows :—

"Torquay.

" DEAREST ARTHUR,

"Your sister is very much worse. The doctor thinks there is no immediate danger, but she is in a critical state. She longs to see you. Come as soon as you can, my dear boy. Bring your wife, if she likes to come.

"Your loving mother,

"A. M. ATHERSTONE."

The unsteady hand, the short, broken sentences, so unlike Lady Atherstone's usually graceful, well-composed epistles, told a tale of sore agitation and anxiety.

"I think you should go," said Lord Trevor, gravely, as he returned the letter.

"Of course, of course ; but the question is, when ? You see Ida never knew my sister. I cannot expect her to feel much about it, or to be ready to give up the ball to-night on her account. I think it would be unreasonable to expect that."

"*Unreasonable* to expect your wife not to go to a ball when your sister is dying ?" burst hotly from Lord Trevor's lips.

" She is not *dying*," said Arthur, hastily. " Give me the Railway Guide, Launcelot ; it is just behind you on that table."

As he hastily ran his eye down the columns of figures, an expression that was almost relief came over his face.

" See here, Launcelot," said he; " I could not go to-night, possibly. The last train leaves at five o'clock, ten minutes from this time. I will go and tell Ida, and if she seems to wish it I can take her with me by the 8.40 to-morrow."

He went upstairs. There stood his wife before the long pier-glass, dressed in a flowing robe of some gauzy white material, made low to show her exquisite neck and arms ; here and there clusters of apple-blossom were placed, their delicate pink contrasting with the pure white. The vain child had put on all her ornaments, and the diamonds flashed in her ears and round her throat as she turned and saw Arthur.

" Well, sir, is not the dress perfect ? Can you suggest any improvement ?"

" You look lovely, my darling, as you

always do. But I want to speak to you about a serious matter, so pay attention for one minute."

"About a serious matter! Oh, dear, what a bore! Can't it be deferred till to-morrow, Arthur? I feel the reverse of serious at this moment."

And she began to execute a few waltz steps before the glass, turning her head to watch the graceful sweep of her long train.

" Come here, Ida, and throw a shawl over your shoulders. You will catch cold."

He took her hand, and led her reluctantly to the sofa, and, seeing there was no help for it, she sat down, saying a little impatiently—

" Don't be long, Arthur; I expect Lady Laura in a few minutes."

Most men would have exclaimed, " Hang Lady Laura !" if indeed they had not used a more forcible expression; but Arthur only replied gently—

"I will not keep you long, dear. I have just heard from my mother, and she says Mary is much worse, in a very 'critical state.'"

"Oh, dear! I am sorry for that; but she has been a long time ill, has she not?"

"Yes; but not like this. I fear she may not recover; and she wishes so much to see me."

"Arthur, you are not going—not to-night, at any rate? Think of the ball!"

The colour rose to Arthur's cheek; the best tempers in the world have their limits, and his were nearly reached.

"I think more of my sister," he said, rather shortly. And then, seeing her look of disappointment, he added, kindly, "You shall go to the ball all the same, dear. Lady Laura will take charge of you; and you will know Trevor and Captain Moncrieff, at any rate. I shall leave by the early train to-morrow."

"But, Arthur, you will go to-night; pray, *pray* say you will. Think how strange it will look if I am there alone, when we have not been married six weeks."

"I would rather not."

"But you will not disappoint me, dear Arthur, for my sake."

A little more pleading and coaxing, and she gained her point. Arthur consented with a heavy heart, and Ida ran gaily downstairs to receive Lady Laura. Somehow it had never even crossed his mind to ask her to accompany him to Torquay on the morrow ; and he could not help feeling a little hurt that she had not even asked when he was likely to return.

" Well, she is but a child," he thought, " and I can't expect her to care much for a person she never saw. My poor, poor Mary !"

So it came to pass that Lord Trevor was amazed that night to behold Mrs. Atherstone enter the ball-room a perfect *blaze* of beauty and jewels (if it is allowable so to apply the word), accompanied by her husband, looking grave and careworn indeed, but evidently making strong efforts to appear cheerful for his wife's sake.

So indignant was his lordship, that he strode up to Ida as she stood near the doorway, and asked her for the first dance, in a suppressedly hostile tone of voice, intend-

ing to take the opportunity of reading her
a lecture.

"I am surprised to see you here to-night,
Mrs. Atherstone," he began, as they took
their places at the head of the quadrille.

"Are you? Did you not know we were
coming?"

"I knew that you *were* coming; but I
imagined that this sad news from Torquay
would have made some difference. Arthur
cannot be in much heart for gaieties."

A flush rose to her fair cheek; she felt
a little conscience-stricken.

"I am afraid it was selfish of me, Lord
Trevor; but I was *so* anxious to come. I
never was at a ball before."

"Could you not have come without vic-
timising Arthur?" was the stern rejoinder.

He was determined not to be mollified,
though her pretty face of penitence, and
the innocent way in which she took all the
blame on herself, would have touched a
harder heart than his.

"Of course I could have come with Lady
Laura," she replied; "but I thought it

would seem so odd—we have been such a short time married."

No answer; and the rest of the quadrille was gone through in dead silence. Ida found herself courteously but coldly handed through the figures, her delicate little fingers held by their extreme tips, while Lord Trevor's stern judicial face would have alarmed a much more hardened sinner than she was.

"I am afraid you think I have been *very* wrong, Lord Trevor," she said, as the last bars of music sounded from the band, and they turned to walk through the rooms.

He looked down, and saw her blue eyes brimming over with tears.

"Poor little soul!" he thought, "it is a shame to spoil her first ball." And he replied, kindly, "You did not *mean* to be selfish, I am sure."

"Indeed I did not; but I am so stupid and thoughtless sometimes. No, Captain Moncrieff, I am not engaged."

And she was borne off, while Lord Trevor leant against a pillar, and watched her graceful form till it disappeared among the dancers.

"She has a good heart, I am convinced," he mused. "How meekly she took all my cool speeches! I suppose I am the only man whom she will dance with to-night that will not overwhelm her with compliments ; and no wonder, she is the loveliest girl I ever saw. She will make Arthur a jewel of a wife, if she is not spoilt."

If she is not spoilt ! Those who watched Ida Atherstone that night (and many eyes, critical as well as friendly, noted her every movement) came soon to the conclusion that she was in a fair way to be spoilt. Her perfect innocence and freshness, and the naïve interest she took in the gay scene (so new to her), proved almost as great an attraction as her exceeding beauty. Mrs. Douglas, the giver of the ball, to use her own expression, "quite fell in love" with her ; for Ida had yet not learnt to have a different set of graces and smiles for ladies and gentlemen, and was equally charming and fascinating to both.

Captain Moncrieff had accomplished his introduction to her two or three days before, and took advantage of this ball to pay desperate court to the young wife, no doubt reckoning on an easy conquest over her apparent simplicity. He followed her everywhere, but in spite of the violent siege he laid to her heart, he did not succeed in making the smallest breach in the fortress. Indeed, she thought him rather a bore than otherwise; and during the evening she frequently cast a glance at Lord Trevor, as he gaily danced and flirted with the young Brightonians, wishing that *he* had been her partner instead.

"It is strange," she thought to herself, "he laughs, and talks, and compliments other women—some of them married women—it is only to me he is grave and severe, *only to me.* He is the only man I know who never makes pretty speeches to me, or seems to care to be with me. Oh bother that Captain Moncrieff, here he is again."

Still it was an evening of intense enjoy-

ment to Ida, and the brilliant success of
her first appearance filled Lady Laura with
delight.

"Oh," remarked that good lady to her
daughter, "if only I had the bringing out
of that girl, she should have secured a
better match than Arthur Atherstone.
With that face and figure, she might have
been a duchess."

The only drawback to Ida's perfect happiness—if we accept Lord Trevor's cold
unfriendliness—was when she glanced at
Arthur. He stood near the door most of
the evening, occasionally exchanging a few
words with a friend, but not dancing at all,
and with a tired, bored look on his face,
which never varied. But when his weary
blue eyes rested on his wife, in her sparkling jewels, and not less sparkling beauty,
he momentarily forgot the sad household
at Torquay, the mourning, heart-broken
mother, the dying sister, and tried to
appear more cheerful, lest his want of
gaiety should cloud hers. At last Ida's
conscience pricked her so unmercifully, that

she went up to him, and laying her white gloved hand on his arm, she whispered,

" Dear Arthur, you *do* look so miserable, let us go home."

" Not really, Ida ; you are not tired yet ?"

" Yes I am, I want to go. I don't want to stay one minute longer. By the bye, what time do you start to-morrow ; you never told me ?"

" By the first train ; I think it leaves at 8.40."

" And I have kept you up all this time. Oh, how selfish I have been ! Get me my cloak, quick, and do order the carriage."

With quite feverish haste she bid adieu to the hostess and Lady Laura, and in five minutes they were driving rapidly back to the hotel.

" Arthur, do you mean to take me to-morrow ?" she asked, when they had reached their own room.

" My darling, do you mean that you wish to come ?"

" I don't like you going away without

14—2

me, and I don't like being here alone," she answered, doubtfully. "But it *is* a long journey to Torquay, and I have a cold. On the whole, I would rather that you decided for me."

"Well, then, Ida, I will decide that you shall remain here till Monday, at any rate; I will come back on that day, and then, if you wish it, you can return with me."

As he expected, her face brightened at once.

"I shall have Lady Laura to walk with," she said, "and Mrs. Douglas has offered to take me out driving any afternoon. But, Arthur, you *will* come back on Monday?"

"If all goes well at home, I promise it."

So the matter was settled. At half-past eight the next morning, Arthur was walking up and down the draughty platform of the Brighton Station. It was a bleak, disagreeable morning, a bitter north-east wind was blowing, and occasionally a light shower of sleet fell. At his second turn he almost ran against a tall, greatcoated, moustached individual, very like himself, and exclaimed,

" Why, Trevor, is it you ?"

" Of course it is ; I have come to see you off. Is not your wife here ?"

" No, poor child, I left her fast asleep. It is far too bitter a morning for her to come out. Well, this is friendly of you, old fellow."

" Not at all, I like it."

The two friends walked up and down, arm-in-arm, occasionally indulging in a vigorous stamp to warm their half-frozen toes.

" I am particularly glad to see you, Trevor," said Arthur, at length, " for there is something I wanted to ask you to do for me."

" All right, fire away; the train will be up in five minutes."

" It is about Ida. You see, I don't half like leaving her alone, even for a few days, she is so unused to it. I dare say Lady Laura and Mrs. Douglas will look after her, but I don't particularly care about her being so very intimate with them."

" Well ?"

" I don't want it to be a tie upon you, but if you could now and then go and see Ida, and be in some way a friend to her. That young Moncrieff plagues her a good deal, and she is so perfectly inexperienced, that she really does not understand how to get rid of a bore."

" I am not sure that I quite understand——"

" Oh, if it would be a bother, don't think of it."

" There now, my dear fellow, don't be huffy ; I will do my best. Only you know Mrs. Atherstone mayn't quite fancy being looked after by me."

" You need not fear any difficulty there, she likes you very much."

" Does she ?"

" Yes, and she knows what old friends you and I have always been. I should like you to know each other *well*. Sometimes,

Trevor, I have fancied that you don't quite take to my wife."

"Indeed, I—I—like her very much. I will do my best, Arthur, indeed I will ; you may rely on me."

Something in his tone of voice made Arthur turn and look at him, but he promptly averted his face.

"I have thought lately that you were not looking well, Trevor. You have seemed rather dull and out of spirits. Does this place suit you ? The air is too strong for some people."

"I am all right, thanks."

"Are you sure ?"

"Well, perhaps I am *not* quite the thing. I think I will try change in a week or so."

The undecided, hesitating tone was so unlike his friend, that Arthur looked at him again with some anxiety. If he had been a woman, he would have taken Lord Trevor's hand, and whispered earnestly, "Confide in me, dearest. We will have no secrets from each other, will we ?" Being a man, he only said quietly,

" If there is anything wrong, you would tell me ?"

" Certainly, of course. Here is the train, Arthur. Have you got your ticket ?"

" Yes ; all right, Good-bye, Trevor, and don't forget my little commission."

" I won't forget. You will be back on Monday ?"

" I hope so. I shall do my best."

The train steamed out of the station, and Lord Trevor walked slowly home. Arthur was right, he *was* changed. The gay spirits that had been so remarkable in him were departed, or only revisited him by fits and starts. The openness and candour which had been the great charm of his manner, had given place to a morose kind of melancholy, and he was growing thin and pale. In every sense of the word he was not the same. Poor young man ! he felt it bitterly himself, and as he walked alone along the Parade, he lifted his hat from his brow, and let the keen wind lift his brown locks and cool his burning forehead, as he muttered to himself, "Some madness possesses me. I must get rid of it, or I shall do some awful wickedness. He has such confidence in me, such complete, inncent trust. Oh, Arthur, Arthur!"

CHAPTER XIII.

"Then fell upon the house a sudden gloom,
A shadow on those features fair and thin;
And softly, from that hushed and darkened room,
Two angels issued, where but one went in."
                                        LONGFELLOW.

OWING to some unavoidable delay, it was late in the afternoon before Arthur reached Torquay. The red December sunset threw a lurid light over the pretty little town, and the rippling sea was turned in some parts to liquid gold, reminding him, with a strange, sudden pang, of the " sea of glass mingled with fire," before which another ransomed spirit would so soon stand.

Lady Atherstone met him in the hall, composed and gentle as ever, though her voice sounded unnaturally hoarse and low as she asked him to come into the dining-room and have some dinner.

"You will be exhausted, my dear boy," she said, anxiously; "you have been travelling and fasting all day."

"No, indeed, mother; I dined on the way. Only a glass of wine and a biscuit, please. Can I go upstairs?"

"Yes, she is quite ready; but she will be distressed that you have had nothing."

"I shall do very well indeed, mother. I only want to see Mary. She is not *much* worse, is she? Tell me."

Lady Atherstone was saved a reply, for at that moment the door opened abruptly, and Sir Henry entered. It seemed to Arthur that the old man was terribly altered. His face was very thin and careworn, there was a nervous twitch round his mouth, and his hand shook as he greeted his son.

"How are you, Arthur—how are you, my boy? You look well—doesn't he, mother?--quite well. Where's your wife? Not come, eh—not come?"

"My dear father, you look tired; pray sit down," replied Arthur, much shocked at the sudden and alarming change in his father's usual tranquil, dignified manner and appearance. "No, Ida is not come; she had a cold, and—and I thought it best not to over-fatigue her, and it is bitter weather, and——"

"Ah! I see; she didn't care to come to a sick house. Gay young thing! No balls and parties here. Natural enough—natural enough."

"Indeed, dear father, she would have come, if I had wished it, to-day, and she is anxious that I should go and fetch her next Monday."

"My dear Arthur, you are not going away next Monday," exclaimed Lady Atherstone in dismay.

"Only for the day, mother, just to fetch Ida. I can't leave her for long, you see; she is so very young, and she is quite alone."

"Of course she wants you back," murmured Sir Henry. "Young wives must be considered before the old parents — aye, before the old parents." And he dragged himself out of the room without another word or look.

Arthur turned to his mother in utter dismay, for the moment even forgetting his sister. "Mother, what is this? What has happened to my father? Why is he so changed?"

"My poor son, we ought not to have kept it from you," replied Lady Atherstone, in a voice half stifled with tears.

"He *has* been ill, then?"

"He has had a slight paralytic seizure. The doctors think it is not a serious case at present, but you see how it has affected him. At times he is scarcely himself."

"When did this take place?"

"Three days ago. He is much better to-day; yesterday he scarcely spoke or moved. Oh! my boy, this is terrible news for you!"

For, wholly overwhelmed by this second calamity, Arthur had sunk down in a chair, covering his face with his hands, his whole frame shaking with suppressed passionate grief. Only for a moment, however; his manly, unselfish nature soon reasserted itself, and he looked up, and met his mother's tranquil, sorrowing eyes.

" Dear mother, forgive me. I ought not to give way; only this is so sudden, so awful ! Let me go to Mary."

He spoke the last words with an earnestness that was almost abrupt. Lady Atherstone smiled, her gentle, heart-broken smile. She, too, knew that Mary's room was the best place for him just then— Mary's sweet face the best cordial to his weary spirit. So she silently led the way, and in another moment Arthur saw his sister once more.

She was lying on her bed, wrapped in a light-blue dressing-gown, her face turned towards the window, so that he only saw at first the small, shapely head, with its soft brown plaits, neat and smooth as ever.

" Mary !"

" Arthur !"

She turned quickly, and he knelt down

by the bed, and threw one arm round her in the old protecting brotherly way.

" My darling, how are you ?—not so *very* ill, after all ?"

She held him close to her, kissing his brow and cheeks with a strange, passionate fervour, unlike the quiet, reserved Mary of old.

" I am *glad* to have seen you, Arthur, my only brother; I could not have died without that."

" *Died!* You are not going to die, Mary ; you—are—not—going—to—die."

The last words were forced out slowly and with difficulty, for, exhausted by the effort of rising from her pillows, Mary lay back panting, her eyes closed, her cheeks white and deathly indeed. Ah ! how sunk they were, those pretty cheeks ! what deep hollows lay beneath the closed eyes ! and with what a visible painful effort the struggling breath came and went. Arthur noted all this with anxious, jealous eyes, almost fearing to speak lest he should disturb her, but in a few minutes she looked up and said—

"I have so much to say to you, Arthur, dear, and as much to ask you. Come a little closer, for I am very weak."

He moved a chair to the side of the bed, and then leant forward, his dark head almost touching her pretty hair, his hand tightly clasped in hers.

"What is it, Mary? Don't try to hurry, dear; tell it me all quietly."

"Well, first about Ida. You will think I am very foolish and superstitious, Arthur, but I have had such strange, sad dreams about you two lately : they have come so often, that they almost seemed like a presentiment. But I know it is all nonsense and nervousness, and I will try to think no more about it if you will just tell me that hitherto you have been *perfectly* happy and satisfied with her. It seems a strange, almost a wrong, thing to ask, Arthur, but you know invalids have their fancies."

She paused suddenly from exhaustion, and for a minute or two there was no sound in the room but her labouring breath, and the soft plash of the waves below. During that momentary interval, many thoughts passed with the rapidity of lightning through Arthur's mind. Had he not lately observed in his wife instances of selfishness, thoughtlessness, even (a severe judge might say), heartlessness, which had both hurt and surprised him? Had her conduct lately been that of a perfectly loving, tender, sympathetic wife? In spite of her beauty, her innocent gaiety, and her bright, winning ways, could he in very truth say that he was "perfectly happy and satisfied" with her. No, his wife was very dear to Arthur, but truth was still dearer. Not even to soothe a dying sister's anxieties could he stain his lips with the shadow of a falsehood. He bent over Mary, and touched her forehead lovingly with his lips, as he gave his somewhat tardy reply.

"There is no cause for you to be anxious about us, dear—about our happiness, I mean. Ida has her faults—who has not?

But she is a good girl on the whole, and my very dear wife."

Something in the tone of those last words caused the hot blood to rush into Mary Atherstone's face as she quickly turned away her head. Hers had not been an unnatural question under the peculiar circumstances, but it had been an unwise one. "If," she thought reproachfully to herself, "if her fears really had some foundation in fact, would not the being compelled to answer them give a definite shape to feelings which would otherwise have remained happily dormant? Why raise suspicions which had so much better be lulled to rest?" Perhaps some of these thoughts reflected themselves in her expressive countenance, for Arthur leant over her again, and said tenderly—

"You are weak, dear Mary, and so you are nervous and fanciful. I wish you could have seen Ida; I hope you *will* see her in a few days. Her sweet face would lay your doubts to rest more effectually than any words of mine could do."

" She is coming to see me then ?"

" I hope to fetch her on Monday."

" I shall not live till Monday, Arthur. Don't interrupt me, dear ; it does me good to talk, and I dare not say a word to mamma. She has enough to bear. Do you know they have promised me to go back to Arling when I am dead ?"

" Have they ?"

The tone of his voice was unnaturally low and calm. Mary glanced at his face, and saw the effort he was making to listen quietly to words which cut him to the heart. She laid her hand lovingly on his, saying—

" I won't say much more, Arthur ; indeed, I *can't*. I only want you to tell me you will remind them of that promise. They dread seeing Arling, for the sake of the sad memories there ; but it is their duty not to forsake the old place. I am told Elizabeth Helmore is working very hard there ; but they want new schools, and——"

She paused again ; and, through the

deepening twilight, Arthur saw that a strange pallor had crept over her face. Much alarmed, he rose to ring the bell; but at the same moment Lady Atherstone entered the room, and beckoned to him to withdraw.

On the stairs he met Sir Henry, making a slow and laborious ascent, pausing at each step to cling to the banisters and gasp for breath, in a way which showed the effect was almost too much for him. Ah! and one short fortnight ago he had mounted those same stairs as easily and almost as briskly as Arthur himself.

"My dear father, you should have called me," said Arthur, offering his strong arm, which was eagerly seized by the feeble old man. "You are not strong enough to climb these steep stairs."

"I was strong enough a few days ago," murmured Sir Henry. "What has changed me so? No, my boy, not that way; I am going to Mary."

"Not just now, dear father. I had to leave her only this minute. She has ex-

hausted herself with talking to me. Come
to your own room."

"Do you wish to keep me from my own
daughter?" was the querulous reply.

But after a little gentle expostulation,
he yielded ; and Arthur took him to his
own room, where he sunk into a chair, and
seemed to fall into a kind of heavy torpid
slumber. There was nothing to be done
for him, and after summoning his own servant, Arthur went to his room and wrote
to Ida.

That night was a heavy, anxious, sleep-
less one to him. Such men as Arthur
Atherstone have very warm family affections ; and though he was well used to sorrow, each successive blow did not fall the
less heavily because it had been preceded
by others.

When the tardy morning broke at length,
and he arose and dressed with the first rays
of daylight, he was startled by the reflection which met him in the glass. Yesterday his eyes had been bright and sparkling
with health, his cheeks had a fresh bloom,

his aspect had been that of a young man in the prime of life, robust, healthy, happy; to-day his face was pale and careworn, his eyes dim and swollen, his pulse weak and fluttering. Years might have passed over his head instead of one single night.

"This will never do," he muttered, angrily, to himself. " I ought to be a support to my mother and Mary; and here I am, as weak and incapable as a girl."

He threw the window wide open, and eagerly inhaled the fresh salt breeze. Then he heard his door gently open, but did not turn round immediately. When he did, a letter lay on the dressing-table, directed in Ida's small, somewhat straggling hand. He tore it open, and read as follows :—

" Brighton.

" DEAREST ARTHUR,

" Is it not good of me to write so soon ? You have not left the house two hours, and here I am scribbling away as eagerly as if we were engaged lovers, instead of *old married people* of nearly two months' standing. I hope you found your father and mother all right, and Mary better. I wish she could have managed her attack a little later, so as not to take you away just now, when I want you so much. Lady Laura has just sent in a note to say that Mrs. Douglas gives an 'at home' to-morrow, and that she will take me if I like to go. I don't know how I shall decide; at present my cold is very bad, my eyes fishy, my nose swollen, and altogether I look *hideous*. Come back on Monday—mind, you *promised*—and if Mary is all right, we need not perhaps go to Torquay for a day or two. Herr Kühe is going to give some grand concerts. The town band has just struck up the 'Blue Danube' outside. I must snatch the opportunity of practising my waltz steps, in which you say I am so backward.

" Your affectionate wife,

" IDA."

Arthur laid down the letter with a heavy

sigh, for which he reproached himself the moment after.

"She is only a child," he thought; "how can I expect her to have the feeling and sympathy of a woman? She does not know how ill Mary really is."

Here another knock came at his door— a hurried, feeble tap. He opened it at once, and there stood Lady Atherstone, her cheeks deadly white, her eyes dry and dilated. She laid her cold, trembling fingers on his arm.

"Come to Mary, Arthur, she wants you."

In another moment he had crossed the narrow passage, and stood by his sister's bed. There she lay, the sweet face calm as ever, scarcely disfigured by the grey pallor which never comes but once on any human countenance, For nearly half an hour she lay thus, silent and motionless, but with the old unchangeable sisterly love beaming in her blue eyes, whenever she turned them on Arthur.

Lady Atherstone had gone to send another message for the doctor. Sir Henry could not be aroused. Only Arthur was there, when, between the long, painful respirations, he caught the words, "I had another dream, Arthur, I can't tell you— but—trust God—it will all come right—" Anxiously he raised her in his arms, and strove to catch the last feeble words, but it was in vain. Even as he watched, the light came over her face which

"Never shone on land or sea,"

and that which he laid down so tenderly on the pillow, was no longer Mary Atherstone.

CHAPTER XIV.

"It is the little rift within the lute
  That by-and-by will make the music mute,
  And, ever widening, slowly silence all."
                              TENNYSON.

ON the afternoon of the day after Arthur's departure, Ida was sitting alone in the hotel, feeling very low spirited and solitary. In truth, she was not quite happy in her mind. No doubt it had *not* been kind to allow Arthur to start alone on his melancholy journey, and, after all, what had she gained by remaining behind?

The sky had clouded over, and it was raining heavily; no chance of a walk or drive to-day, very little chance even of a visitor. "Suppose this weather should continue, suppose Arthur should be de-

tained at Torquay beyond Monday, how
dreary and desolate Brighton would become. Arling itself could not be much
duller."

"I do think Lord Trevor might call to-
day," she murmured to herself. "Men
don't mind rain, and Arthur said he would
be sure to come and see me. That is one
blessing of being a married woman, one can
receive gentleman visitors without a chape-
rone. Well, if he *did* call, I don't know
that he would be much amusement; he
says very little, and is always stern and
grave with *me*. It is very odd; I suppose
it must be my stupid shyness that makes
him feel awkward and constrained. Ah!
who is that?"

A tall figure, clad in a long mackintosh,
sleek and shiny with the wet, was struggling along the King's Road, engaged in a
desperate endeavour to hold an umbrella
against the boisterous wind, which blew
furiously in his face, and at the same time
avoid running foul of any other luckless
pedestrian. So effectually did his dress

disguise him, that Ida could not be certain if she knew him, though she was not much surprised when, a moment after, "Lord Trevor" was announced, and she saw the dark, handsome face, so bright and engaging to others, so cold and unsympathetic only to *her*. He shook hands with his usual stiff formality, and took a seat at some distance from her sofa.

"It is a miserable day, Mrs. Atherstone. I suppose you have not attempted to go out ?"

"No, not at present ; but it is so awfully dull here all alone, that I had serious thoughts of putting on a waterproof, and having a fight with the elements. You are very wet, Lord Trevor."

"Oh, it does not signify, thanks ; I never mind rain. I do not remember ever catching cold in my life."

"Really ! You must be a very fortunate person."

"I believe I am."

Silence. Ida looked down, and began to fidget with her rings ; his lordship gazed out of the window at the dismal, foggy prospect, and racked his brains for something to say. Of course the lady spoke first, and equally, of course, her observation had better have been left unsaid.

"I am afraid you find my society very depressing, Lord Trevor. We never seem to have anything to say to each other, do we?"

He looked up hastily, and a close observer might have noted a strange, pained look in his dark eyes, as he replied,

"On the contrary, Mrs. Atherstone, it is I who am to blame. Every one pronounces you a most amusing companion, but I have been very dull lately. I think I am not quite well. You must excuse my stupidity; we do not meet often."

"But I see you talking quite gaily to other people," continued Ida, who, like all her sex, never knew how to leave well alone. "It is not very complimentary to me, Lord Trevor, you always seem *bored* in my society."

His cheek flushed, and taking an ivory

paper cutter from the table, he began to
turn it nervously about in his fingers.

"I do not feel bored in your society,
Mrs. Atherstone," he said after a short
pause, speaking in a measured formal tone,
"I am very far from feeling that, as you
must know."

"I know nothing of the kind," she said,
in a pettish voice, like a discontented child.

"Witness my coming to see you this
pouring wet day, I will answer for it you
will have no other visitor."

"Well, that is a charitable action certainly," and she threw herself back on the
sofa cushion, and sighed wearily. "I do
hate bad weather—days when one cannot
get out, I hate them even when Arthur is
with me, for though he does his best to
amuse me, he has absolutely *no* conversation, as I dare say you know."

She was tired and a little out of humour,
or she had not spoken in this way, but her
visitor did not seem disposed to make any
allowances.

"Arthur used to be a capital companion,"

he said dryly, "he can talk intelligently on almost any subject."

"Oh, no doubt! but don't you know there are days when he does not want to talk *intelligently*, days when one would rejoice in

> ' A creature not too bright and good
> For human nature's daily food.'

Some one for instance like Captain Moncrieff, who would rattle away and keep one amused. Or—such a companion as I think *you* could be, Lord Trevor, if you only let yourself be natural." And she glanced at him saucily out of her merry blue eyes. The paper-knife in Lord Trevor's hand snapped in half.

"Never mind," said Ida, negligently, in reply to his somewhat unnecessarily profuse apologies, "it is not real ivory."

"It was very careless. I have a way of fidgeting with things. If I can be of any use to you during Arthur's absence, Mrs. Atherstone, I hope you will let me know. You have my address."

He rose to go.

" Are you tired of me so soon ?" she replied, making no attempt to rise, but glancing up at him with smiling, sleepy eyes. " Do you know how long your visit has lasted ? Just six minutes."

His expression did not change ; he did not even make the plausible excuse that most men would have done. Yet that sweet pleading face would have tempted most men to linger ; even the dull, foggy atmosphere, so fatal to the appearance of most fair persons, could not succeed in dimming her radiant beauty. No sculptured Venus, no pictured houri, could look more enchanting than Ida Atherstone in that negligent graceful attitude ; but apparently she made no favourable impression on her visitor. He held out his hand, saying courteously but coldly—

" I must go now, Mrs. Atherstone. I have a good deal to do. Have you any commissions in the town ?"

" If you are going anywhere near Treacher's Library, will you change these books for me ?   I want the third volume."

He took the novels from her hand, and his face changed as he saw the title.

"This is a clever authoress, Mrs. Atherstone ; but her works are scarcely edifying. Does Arthur know you have read this ?"

"I don't know.   I don't suppose he would care."

"I do not think he would approve of it. I will get you something else."

And before she had sufficiently recovered her astonishment to expostulate, he was gone.

"Well, of all cool proceedings," exclaimed the young lady, "that is the coolest I ever heard of.   How amused Arthur would be !   It is positively the first time I ever saw his lordship the least interested in anything that concerned me."

At that moment the door again opened, and a servant entered with a salver, on which lay an ominous-looking envelope, directed in large and flourishing letters. Ida opened it hastily, and stood in dismay, the colour forsaking her cheeks, as she surveyed a formidable row of figures, amounting in all to £47 17s.

It was the bill for her ball-dress and other articles for the toilette, which had been purchased under the surveillance and by the advice of Lady Laura. The amount might not have seemed outrageous to an experienced woman of fashion, but to Ida, who had never in her life had a dress which cost more than five pounds, it appeared simply appalling.

After a moment's hesitation, she flew upstairs, tossed on her hat and cloak, and, forgetful alike of wind and rain and her usual nervous dislike to going out alone, flew along the moist, slippery bricks to Lady Laura's house.

So it came to pass that the good lady was roused from her comfortable afternoon siesta by the appearance of a forlorn, dripping figure, with scared, woe-begone face, who rather sunk into than seated herself in the chair offered to her, and incontinently burst into tears.

"My dear girl, what is the matter?" exclaimed her ladyship, in much alarm. "Have you had bad news from Arthur? Try and speak calmly, and don't sob so; you will make yourself ill."

"I have had no bad news from Arthur; but oh, Lady Laura, look at this! What *am* I to do? How can I tell him how wicked I have been, and just now, when he is in such anxiety?"

Lady Laura took the bill from her outstretched hand, and the slightest possible expression of contempt passed over her features as she surveyed the amount.

"My dear Ida, you must be nervous this afternoon," she remarked, coolly. "No doubt, for a simple country clergyman's daughter, this bill would have been extravagant; but you must remember your position is very different now. Your husband could afford to pay twice the amount every month if you asked him; and he would do so gladly, I am sure. Whatever faults he may have, Arthur Atherstone never was mean."

"But, Lady Laura, this is not my only bill. There was that sealskin jacket you persuaded me to buy the other day, which cost fourteen pounds."

"Well, and very reasonable too. I call that jacket a perfect bargain."

"And the hat with those long ostrich plumes, and the silver chatelaine, and the inlaid writing-desk! Oh, it is perfectly *awful!* I shall never dare to tell Arthur. What would Elizabeth say?" And she buried her face in her hands, and sobbed bitterly.

Lady Laura yawned; she was getting a little bored.

"I must say this excessive grief is un-called for," she said, languidly. "I do not admit that you have been extravagant; and even if you *have*, a little lavish expen-diture is always excusable in a young bride. You need not even tell Arthur, unless you choose. I suppose he gives you an ample allowance?"

"He has said nothing about that yet; he has always paid my bills himself."

"Oh, dear ! that is a very uncomfortable plan. You must get him to let you have a fixed sum every year—it ought to be five hundred pounds, at least, with his fortune. Here is Rogers with the tea. You must have a cup, my dear ; you are nervous and depressed, and so imagine all sorts of miseries."

Lady Laura's confident tone partly restored Ida's equanimity. She dried her tears, and endeavoured to appear more cheerful, more especially as she discerned, with a woman's unerring tact, that her friend was more inclined to be bored than sympathising.

Alda came into the room just as Ida was rising to take her leave, and shook hands in the peculiarly shrinking, nervous manner which always succeeded in arousing her mother's ire. The young girl had conceived a romantic admiration for the beautiful young wife ; but this did not tend to make her more talkative. On the contrary, she preferred to establish herself in a distant corner of the room, and gaze at her idol—

"Her rapt soul sitting in her eyes ;"

or, as Lady Laura less poetically described it, like a *stuck pig*.

"Will you allow your daughter to come to tea with me some day, Lady Laura?" asked Ida, good-naturedly. "I shall be quite alone till Monday, and it would be a great pleasure to me to see her."

"Alda has no conversation, and is the stupidest companion in the world," replied her affectionate parent. "Don't look so amazed, my dear Ida. She knows it perfectly well herself; I tell her so twenty times a day. She is not lively by nature, and she makes no effort to improve. However, if you are good-natured enough to wish to have her, she may go."

"Would you like to come and see me?" said Ida, sweetly, turning to the poor girl, who had blushed till she could blush no longer, and seemed on the verge of tears.

"Oh, thank you so much! I—I should

be so pleased—so—" mumble, mumble. The rest of her eager reply was inaudible.

"There, you have stammered enough," said her mother, contemptuously. "Mrs. Atherstone will excuse your saying more. You shall go on Sunday—if that is convenient to you, Ida?"

"Indeed, I shall be very pleased to see her," replied Ida, moving towards the door.

"One moment, my dear," said Lady Laura, making a quick sign to her daughter, which caused her to vanish through a side-door with a celerity born of long habit. "My servant will fetch you a cab; you can't walk home in these torrents of rain. Now take my advice, Ida, and don't worry yourself about these bills. When you have had a little more experience, you will laugh at your own foolishness in allowing such trifles to disturb your tranquillity."

"If you think I could manage without telling Arthur."

"Of course, if you are nervous about it that is easily done. Ask him to let you

have an allowance, and pay these accounts
with the first instalment."

"Thank you for that suggestion, Lady
Laura, you are so good to me. I shall
certainly follow your advice."

"There is a good child. I shall come and
see you on Monday. Here is your cab.
Good-bye, and don't let me see such a panic-
struck face again for the sake of a few
paltry bills."

Ida drove off, feeling considerably cheered
by the judicious mixture of irony and sympathy contained in Lady Laura's words.
The bills were straightway locked up in
her desk, to be paid when Arthur should
return home. Nevertheless, there was a
certain weight of anxiety at her heart
which lay there heavy as lead, and was
not materially lightened even by the con-
soling reflection that all ladies of any
pretensions to fashion went into debt, and
that it was a mark of inferior and country
breeding, to be guilty of the anomaly of
paying one's way.

On her table she found a few lines from

Arthur, briefly announcing his sister's death, and ending with the words,

" I shall hope to return to Brighton on Thursday or Friday next, but it is impossible quite to fix the day. I am sorry to disappoint you, my darling, but after the funeral I have persuaded my father and mother to leave at once for Arling, and I cannot feel happy about them till I see them comfortably settled at the Grange. I hope by the middle of January we shall all be there for the rest of the winter."

Must it be confessed that Ida's first feelings on reading this letter, were those of annoyance rather than of grief. Of course it was very sad about poor Mary, and no doubt Lady Atherstone was much overcome, but she had a husband to take care of her. Why on earth should they insist on Arthur's remaining away ?

" There is no doubt," said the young lady decidedly, replacing the letter in the envelope with a gesture expressive of much irritation. " There is no doubt it is a great bore to marry a man who is afflicted

with delicate family connections. Arthur
says his father is very much altered, most
likely *he* will be the next to give way, and
want his son to go and nurse him, and then
probably my dear mother-in-law will suc-
cumb, and so it will go on for ever. Arthur
has the most exaggerated idea of his duty
as a son, and they seem to have no scruple
in trespassing on his good nature. As for
spending the winter at Arling with two
sick old people, I simply will not do it. I
can just fancy it, father with the rheumatism, Elizabeth racing about the village all
day with blankets and beef-tea, Sir Henry
groaning in one corner of the fire-place with
gout, and Lady Atherstone in the other
with neuralgia, while Arthur will go about
with a face like a mute at a funeral. That
is not what I married for. No, no, London
is the place for me, and to London we will
go. Arthur will do anything I ask him
with a little coaxing."

No doubt in ordinary matters, but where
duty was concerned, the young wife had
yet to learn that Arthur could be as im-

movable as a rock. Ah, what a revelation those last words of hers would have been to his unsuspicious nature, "*That is not what I married for.*"

CHAPTER XV.

" Fair tresses man's imperial race ensnare
And beauty draws us with a single hair."
                                        POPE.

SUNDAY morning rose bright and glorious.
The Brighton climate differs from other
English towns in this respect, it generally
either rains or shines, it very seldom *sulks*.
The dwellers in this delightful watering-
place may indeed be subjected occasionally
to the infliction of a pouring wet day, but
they are spared the long weeks of gloomy
weather which have inspired foreigners
with such a righteous horror of our English
autumns, weeks when the sun seems to
have snugly rolled himself up in a thick
impervious blanket of clouds, and obsti-
nately refuses to show himself.

The brilliant weather, cold and frosty as
it was, had a cheering effect on Ida's somewhat depressed spirits, and she determined
to take advantage of the fine morning to
walk to St. Michael's church, about half a
mile distant from the hotel, and situated
at the top of a very steep hill. She was
looking very pretty to-day. A black
velvet costume trimmed with sable fur
suited her fair complexion admirably, and
her wavy hair shone like gold in juxta-
position with a charming little blue velvet
bonnet, one of Lady Laura's choice. Many
people turned to look after her as she
mounted the steep flight of steps leading
up to the church ; the attention she excited tinged her cheeks with crimson, and
she began to regret not having brought a
maid with her. It was no easy matter to
obtain a seat, as every visitor to Brighton
well knows. The careful and admirable
manner in which the Anglican service is
performed at St. Michael's, renders it one
of the most popular churches in the town.
Ida stood irresolute in the doorway,

scarcely knowing whether it was any use to try and press up the crowded aisle, when a low voice sounded in her ear,

"I have the use of two sittings here, Mrs. Atherstone ; will you follow me ?"

It was Lord Trevor, who walked quickly up the church without waiting to hear her eager thanks, and showed her into an excellent seat, just under the pulpit. When she rose from her knees she glanced round expecting to see him by her side, but he was not there, and after a few minutes she caught sight of his dark head towering above the others in a seat near the door, in the middle aisle.

"So, he will not even sit next me in church," was her mortified reflection, and true enough the chair next to her own remained unoccupied till the beginning of the psalms, when it was appropriated by some weary stranger. How truly it has been said :

"Not e'en the tenderest heart and next our own
Knows half the reasons why we smile or sigh,"

and how far less can we guess at the secret

known to us, by their outward actions.
Little did Ida imagine how often during
the service Lord Trevor's sad dark eyes
wandered to her golden head; and how
often those next to him observed him start
and flush as some movement on her part
brought the fair profile into view. The
reader has probably by this time guessed
Lord Trevor's secret.

From the day that he first saw Ida
Helmore driving her pretty restive pony
in the little town of Daylesford, her image
had taken strong possession of his mind,
and the unavoidably frequent, though
formal, intercourse of the last few weeks
had completed the enchantment so in-
auspiciously begun. It was this fatal
secret which was wearing out his young
manhood, filling his heart with a wild
despair and remorse which at times almost
drove him to frenzy.

At the age of thirty-two he had never
yet felt anything approaching to a serious
attachment for any woman on earth, and
now his pent-up affections flowed in

an overwhelming torrent which almost
threatened at times to undermine his in-
tellect.   Sometimes it seemed to him a
strange awful nightmare, a catastrophe too
abhorrent to be possible that he should
have fallen in love with the wife of his
dearest friend, Arthur, the companion of
his boyhood, he who had taken the place
of a brother to him since the days when
they had played together as little children.
What could he do ? he sometimes asked
himself wearily, how break the fascination
that bound him ?   " What could he do ?"
I hear some indignant reader exclaim, " why
did he not leave Brighton without an hour's
delay, and put hundreds of miles of land
and sea between him and the sweet face
that was luring him to his destruction ?"

Ah, my friend, have *you* always fled
so promptly from temptation ? have *you*
always dashed away the sparkling cup
when it was displayed, glittering and
radiant, before your thirsty lips ? Have *you*
ever turned your back on paradise, and fled
away out into the howling wilderness for

fear lest the shadow of a sin should stain
the white purity of your soul ? If so, you
may sit in judgment on Launcelot Trevor,
not unless. A more generous chivalrous
soul than his never existed ; at this time
he would have cut off his right hand, or
thrown himself deliberately into the sea,
sooner than have spoken a word to Arthur's
wife which might not have been heard and
approved by Arthur himself. Nay, more,
he strove hard to convince himself that
Ida was not worthy to have inspired any
strong affection in the heart of a good man.

Over and over again he assured himself
that she was (as he once told Captain Moncrieff) a "mere pretty doll," incapable of
any deep feeling or generous sentiment,
and over and over again had one glance of
her blue eyes, one pressure of her soft hand
sent all these disparaging thoughts to the
winds and again forced him into a slavery
as abject as it was unwilling. Earnestly
he resolved (and the resolve needed to be
many times renewed) to be as markedly
cold in his manner to his fair idol as was

compatible with courtesy, and as we have
seen, he had hitherto managed to carry out
this resolution with tolerable success. But
oh, if there is a sin in the sight of Almighty
God, which is *sure* in the end to bring disgrace and misery on the offender, it is that
daring obstinacy and pride which refuses
to take warning by the example of count-
less hapless ones who have striven to walk
the same slippery path, and while praying
every day with his lips that he may not be
led " into temptation," advances wilfully so
near the edge of the fatal precipice that it
needs but a chance unexpected word or
look to hurl him over.

The service proceeded, and Ida's attention was gradually drawn away from her
own private vexations by the exceeding
beauty of the music, and still more by the
energetic talent and force of a sermon such
as that favoured congregation often hear,
but which struck her as something marvellous after her father's excellent but simple discourses.

As the congregation filed down the narrow aisle to the sound of a parting voluntary, solemn (yet cheerful) such as that part of the music always should be, Ida looked out for Lord Trevor, but he was nowhere to be seen. Her eyes fell instead on Lady Laura, who waited for her at the bottom of the steps, and the two ladies walked together down Montpelier Road. Her ladyship did not seem in the best of humours. After her first greeting, she walked along silently for some minutes (a most unusual proceeding for her), and then asked somewhat abruptly—

" Is Arthur coming back on Monday ?"

" No ; I am sorry to say he will be detained for some days longer on account of poor Mary's death. She died the day after he arrived there."

" Dear me, how very sad ! I feel for poor Lady Atherstone ; but I suppose there has been no hope for a long time. You will have to go into mourning, Ida."

" Yes ; I must get my things to-morrow. Oh, Lady Laura, *more* bills !"

" Nonsense, my dear, your husband can

well afford to pay them. I have never seen you at St. Michael's before. You do not usually go there ?"

" No ; but I thought I should like the walk this lovely morning."

" Lord Trevor was very civil in offering his seat."

" Yes ; I wished to have thanked him again, but he has vanished somewhere among the crowd."

" Ah, just as well, perhaps," was the mysterious reply.

" Why ?" asked Ida, innocently.

" Well, my dear, you are very young and inexperienced, and you must just let me give you a hint. You have been seen a good deal about with Lord Trevor ; and though he is a young man of most excellent character, it would be as well if people did not notice you were much together during your husband's absence. Brighton is the most gossiping place on the face of the earth ; it is the reason that I made up my mind never to live here."

" I do not understand you, Lady Laura.

Lord Trevor is a great friend of Arthur's, and so he sometimes joins us in our walks, but his manner to me is always particularly distant; indeed, quite remarkably so."

"Well, I am glad to hear that. You see, Ida, it would really be a pity if he was to take any absurd fancy into his head for you, a married woman. I am not afraid of any flirtation on his part, for he is a very honourable, highly-principled man, but it might prevent his marrying, and he really *ought* to marry now. It is a magnificent property, and he would make an admirable husband." She stopped rather abruptly.

A slight flush rose to Ida's brow. She did not really care about Lord Trevor, but he puzzled her a good deal, and interested her still more. She was beginning to entertain just that sort of feeling for him which did not amount to much more than friendship, and which yet made the idea of his marriage not quite an agreeable one to her. But she said nothing, and Lady Laura proceeded, confidentially laying her hand on her companion's arm.

"I feel that I am safe in entrusting a little secret of my own to you, Ida. I have known Lord Trevor's family intimately for some years, though I never met him till this autumn. Last year his sister, Lady Jane, said to me, àpropos of her]brother's settlement in life, 'What an excellent wife your Alda would make for Launcelot!' It was said half in joke, but the idea took root in my mind, and was the real cause of my coming down to Brighton this autumn when I heard his lordship was likely to be here."

"But, Lady Laura, Alda is so *very* young."

"Only one year younger than you, and she looks much older"—(this was a fiction on her ladyship's part). "They have met twice at Mrs. Douglas's, and Alda thinks him very agreeable. If I could only be sure that the admiration was mutual——"

"You would miss her dreadfully, Lady Laura, your only child."

"My dear girl, her marriage would re-

joice me beyond measure. She is no companion to me, we don't get on as well as we
might; she is—well, I don't know how to
express it—not the least *sympathetic* with
me. I find many mothers make the same
complaint of their daughters."

" You treat her as if she was a child."

" Yes, I do that on principle ; I have no
idea of being domineered over by my own
daughter."

Ida thought there was little chance of
the meek, undemonstrative Alda ever attempting to "domineer" over any one, but
she made no reply, and Lady Laura turned
off to the right at the bottom of the hill,
crying, as she shook hands,

" Of course the little secret I have told
you will be kept *quite* to yourself, dear Ida.
Very likely it may all come to nothing, and,
in any case, I should not like to have it
supposed that I have been *manœuvring* to
bring it about. You know I am the last
person in the world to do *that*."

" Of course not."

" Only, my dear, I thought I would just

give you a hint, in case Lord Trevor should seem inclined to pay you any particular attention. It *might* so occur, you know. Good-bye."

Ida walked quickly home, conscious of a certain undefinable uneasiness, caused by Lady Laura's words, but feeling considerably more annoyed with herself for being annoyed.

" The whole world seems to have entered into a conspiracy to worry me," she thought irritably to herself, while taking off her bonnet. " Lady Laura is very absurd, and rather impertinent. As for Lord Trevor ever falling in love with that plain, half-idiotic Alda, the idea is too ridiculous. It is a cruel thing to put it into the girl's head."

About five o'clock Miss Marjoribanks made her appearance, and Ida received her kindly, but with more distance of manner than was usual with her. The poor girl was by no means surprised at this. She had been so often told by her mother that she was the most stupid and wearisome companion in the world; that she had almost ceased to hope that her presence could be anything but an unmitigated bore to any one, and her affectionate gratitude to Ida for condescending to endure her sole company for an hour or two, was something quite touching to behold. Her gentle humility of manner soon thawed her young hostess, and before they parted the two became excellent friends.

A clever modern authoress declares, in one of her latest works, that she finds it difficult to account for the origin of the religious supposition entertained by most people, of a state of future punishment for sin, as, according to her experience of life, every offence is chastised with prompt and extreme severity during our present state of existence.

However this may be, the converse is certainly true. No *good* deed—were it only the saying of a kind word, or the gift of a cup of water—ever passes without its reward in this life, often immediate, but always certain, and one which can be definitely traced to its cause.

Ida's small act of good nature in asking Alda Marjoribanks to spend the afternoon with her, had an immediate beneficial effect in rendering her more cheerful and calm, for, when freed from her mother's chilling presence, the young girl proved anything but a dull companion, and talked with a surprising amount of good sense, and even humour.

Alda had grown up under the depressing sense of being hopelessly misunderstood, and her want of personal advantages had so preyed on her mind, that had it not been for the intervention of a few kind friends, she might have become hopelessly melancholy. Some people think that conceit is the besetting sin common to most young girls ; we are inclined to believe, on the contrary, that a certain half-morbid, half-nervous sense of deficiency in mind, manners, or appearance (often entirely without any just foundation), is a far more common and dangerous foe.

Conceit is pretty sure to be cured in time, as the "Country Parson" truly remarks. Whatever strong shoots of self-sufficiency may develope themselves in youth, the keen pruning-knife used by the world will surely and rudely lop them off, or reduce them to an insignificant size, but a want of due appreciation of ourselves is a more subtle and insidious enemy, more dangerous, because less open.

Never in her life had Ida done a kinder act than when she encouraged Alda's art-less confidences, and, as we have said, the good action met with its corresponding reward. She went to rest that night, dis-posed to take a more lively view of her prospects in life, even should they involve a long winter spent at Arling Grange.

She wrote a few lines to Arthur, to be despatched by the early post, ending with these words :

"Lord Trevor gave me a seat at St. Michael's this morning, which was very civil and attentive of him, especially as it seems he so dislikes a lady's company in church, that he declined to sit next me, and betook himself to a wretched place near the door, where he could have heard little, and seen less. He seems to have a horror of my company, which is certainly not flattering, as he can talk well enough to other people. I am a little *huffy* on the subject, and you may tell him so if you like.

"Your affectionate wife,

"IDA."

CHAPTER XVI.

"Men only weak
Against the charm of beauty's powerful glance."
MILTON.

AT Arling, matters were not progressing quite as favourably as might be desired. Mr. Helmore was laid up with his usual winter foe, rheumatism, and Elizabeth had verified the predictions of all her friends, and worked so hard, early and late, in all sorts of weathers, that her health had also given way, and she was confined to the house by incessant and agonizing attacks of neuralgia.

An enormous and unprecedented amount of work had therefore fallen on the shoulders of the young curate, and as he utterly re-

fused either to abandon any of his philan-
thropic designs, or commit their direction
into less competent hands, the strain upon
him was almost more than his strength
could bear.

No one hated idleness more than Elizabeth, but necessity owns no law, and for
more than a fortnight she was totally
unable to stir from the house, or to
transact any business which required much
head work. Unfortunately the weather continued to be very trying; bleak east winds
alternated with heavy storms of hail and
snow, and these were succeeded by dense
fogs, drenching far more effectually than
the heaviest rain, and rendering the little
sheep paths, which led to the cottages on
the Down, very dangerous, and sometimes
quite impracticable. It was on one of
these dismal afternoons that the melancholy
party from Torquay arrived at the Grange.
Years might have passed over Sir Henry's
head instead of a few months since he last
trod that familiar threshold. His noble
white head was now so bowed that he

seemed to have lost some inches in height, and his once keen blue eye was now dim, and he wandered through the familiar rooms with a vacant, yet yearning glance, which nearly overcame his wife's composure. There was not a dry eye among the crowd of assembled domestics as Lady Atherstone passed through the hall, dignified and erect as ever, but with cheeks as white as the handkerchief she held in her hands, and pale compressed lips, telling of the sore grief within.

" Surely few have been tried as my lady has," said old Mrs. Drury the housekeeper, over her tea that evening, " it is grievous to think on. Five children buried now, and as fine a family as you would wish to see; all such healthy beautiful babies. I can't believe sometimes that Mr. Arthur is the only one left of them all, and his was by no means the strongest constitution when he was a little boy. There's a look in his eyes now sometimes that I don't half like."

" He don't look strong to my mind

neither," remarked Sarah, the under house-maid, "and I doubt if that bright colour is altogether right. 'Tis too much like them beautiful red apples that is never sound within."

"You know nothing about it, Sarah Dawkins," retorted the housekeeper sharply, "'tis like you to be always croaking about something or other."

"'Twas yourself that alluded to the subject first, Mrs. Drury," was the humble answer; "I'm sure I trust we may both be wrong. And the captain has got a young wife to look after him now, 'tis to be hoped she'll be a comfort in the family, pretty dear."

"They do say she is as beautiful as the dawn," remarked Thomas, the under-foot-man, a poetical individual, and a new arrival.

"That she is," was Mrs. Drury's warm reply.

"The loveliest complexion you ever see," said Sarah.

"And the beautifullest hair, just like

threads of gold," added the housekeeper, glancing regretfully at her own sparse grey locks, "much the same as mine was when I was a girl."

Here certain pantomimic gestures, expressive of diversion and incredulity, passed between the footman and Sarah, which unfortunately caught the eye of the elder lady, and caused the instant dispersal of the tea-party.

Upstairs the scene was very different. Sir Henry sat in his favourite easy-chair, the green-shaded reading-lamp standing by a table at his side, just as Arthur always remembered to have been the custom since the days of his childhood, but though the newspapers and periodicals were all arranged as usual, ready to his hand, he made no attempt to look at any of them, but gazed into the fire all the evening with a weary listless air.

Lady Atherstone reclined on the sofa, her head turned away from the light, as though to hide the tears that occasionally escaped from her closed eyelids, and traced their furrows down the wan, thin cheek. Arthur sat by the table, making a pretence of reading, but in reality his eyes seldom wandered from this sad picture, while he tried to fancy how different it would all look when Ida would be sitting there; surely she would come like a sunbeam into this gloomy place, with her sweet face and sunny, winning ways!

The effect of his meditations was to in-duce him to delay no longer in going to fetch his wife, and he communicated this idea to his parents before they separated for the night. He proposed leaving for Brighton the next morning, and bringing Ida back on the afternoon of the same day. But a new and unexpected difficulty arose. Nothing would induce Sir Henry to part with his son, even for a single day, or half a day.

Hoping that a good night's rest would dissipate this unreasonable fancy, Arthur said no more that night; but when he renewed the subject next morning at break-fast, the old man was as unpersuadable as ever, and finally declared that if it was absolutely necessary for his son to go to Brighton, he would go with him.

Of course this idea could not be entertained for a moment, and poor Lady Atherstone was in despair. It was finally settled that Sir Henry could not be crossed, and Arthur sat down with a heavy heart to tell Ida that she must manage the hour-and-a-half's journey by herself, and he would meet her at the station. He had an idea that she would be somewhat annoyed by this arrangement, but he little imagined the storm of indignation with which his letter was received. Already somewhat disposed to think herself neglected, Ida now proved herself fully as unreasonable as Sir Henry, without his excuse of old age and infirmity; and after a fit of passion, which it was as well that no one witnessed except her own maid, threw herself on the sofa, and cried till she made herself absolutely ill.

Such was the scene which met Lord Trevor's eye as he looked in for a cup of

18—2

afternoon tea, to which Ida had invited him, and which appointment she had very naturally forgotten.

As he was announced Ida rose from the sofa, and he stood in dismay at the melancholy spectacle—the pretty blue eyes red and swelled, and the fair hair hanging in most "admired disorder," making her look like a naughty passionate child.

Forgetting for a moment his usual cautious reserve of manner, he hurried forward and took the trembling little hand in his with much sympathy.

"My dear Mrs. Atherstone, what is the matter? have you had any bad news?"

In reply she handed him Arthur's letter. He read it once, twice, and then looked up with a puzzled expression.

"I do not understand. Is this all?"

"*All!* is it not enough?" burst from the offended young matron. "I told Arthur in my last letter that I could not and would not spend the winter at Arling, and now he writes without a word of explanation or apology, just to tell me to come at once, and *alone.* I, who at home was never even allowed to take a walk by myself! I think the whole family must be going mad."

" I am sure that Arthur would not cross your wishes without great cause; you see how very ill Sir Henry is."

" I don't believe a word of it; it is just an excuse."

" I must say, Mrs. Atherstone, that I think you are a little unreasonable."

" Oh! of course; I did not expect any sympathy from *you.*"

Lord Trevor felt sorely puzzled. His own womenkind were remarkably sensible and gentle. Never in his life had he been obliged to encounter that most unreasonable of human beings—a young wife who fancies herself neglected. However, his natural good sense dictated the only course which could prove effectual. He did not attempt to argue the matter, but after a few minutes' silence, during which Ida sobbed without restraint, he said gently—

" This is not a very formidable journey, Mrs. Atherstone; there are. no changes.

Would it make it more comfortable for you if I accompanied you as far as Thurleswood? It is the station just before Arling. I have a friend there who would give me luncheon, and I could return here the same day."

"Oh! Lord Trevor, how *very* kind; but I could not ask such a thing."

"It would be no trouble; I intended to go to Thurleswood some day soon."

(It may be hoped that this last asseveration was pardoned on account of its good nature, but it certainly belonged to the genus called *white lies*.)

"If that is really the case, Lord Trevor, it would of course be a great comfort to me. You have no idea what a baby I am about travelling; many a child knows better how to manage than I do."

"Arthur does not know that."

"No, and pray don't tell him; I should not like him to think me the incapable goose I really am."

And her good humour having fully returned, the two sat down to their tea on friendly and comfortable terms.

In truth, during the last few days Lord Trevor had been persuading himself that he had been erring lately on the side of over-caution almost amounting to incivility, and he told himself that this line of action must not be pursued too far.

"She must not suppose that I wish to avoid her," was his secret argument, "or she will wonder *why*."

Indeed, so far had he reasoned and schooled himself, that he began almost to doubt the existence of his own great love, after all. Perhaps it was only a wild, delirious fancy, such as has sometimes seized men for most unlikely objects; perhaps it might pass away with more familiar intercourse, and he would have "disquieted himself in vain."

"Alas! like some fatal diseases, love is often most severely experienced by those who are unaware of their own hopeless condition. Lord Trevor should have known himself to be no weak and fanciful dreamer, no wild enthusiast; his temperament was not even as poetical and romantic as

Arthur's. In healthy, sound, practical natures like his, love takes deep root, and grows with a hardy vigour which only the icy frost of death can check. But such thoughts as these were far from his mind just now, and he talked and laughed with his fair hostess in a manner which was not much more delightful to him than it was to her.

You might have seen the sparkle of gratified vanity in her eyes as the time passed on, and her hitherto stiff-mannered and indifferent cavalier showed no sign of weariness, but continued to chat away with an easy *abandon* which he had never given way to before in her presence. When he chose, Lord Trevor could be a most delightful companion ; his conversation was sparkling, and his wit at once pointed and refined. No wonder that Ida heaved a deep sigh (not unobserved by him) as he rose to go, and she was left to pass a long, dull evening alone. And can you not believe that these moments of unrestrained intercourse were sweet beyond measure, more

intoxicating than the wildest, brightest
dreams to the man whose heart was filled
with so great a love, a love which grew
every moment in force and intensity, though
he still honestly believed that he was doing
no harm, and, indeed, only performing a
charitable and kindly action in endeavouring to while away one of the solitary hours
spent by Arthur's young wife. Perhaps
few men of his age and temperament, and
under his peculiar circumstances of temptation, would have refrained, at any rate, from
indulging in a few complimentary phrases
during that hour of private and free intercourse, but here Lord Trevor was firm. Not
one glance even of admiration did Ida win
from him ; not one sentence did he utter
which might be construed into a sentiment warmer than friendship. He talked
brilliantly and well, but managed to steer
clear of all dangerous and delicate topics
with a wisdom and astuteness worthy of a
practised diplomate, in spite of the many
traps laid for him by his fair auditor. But

in spite of all his caution, he did not escape undetected.

Ah, my soft-hearted and diplomatic young friend, fresh from Sandhurst or the University, never believe, in spite of all your feigned indifference and studied coldness, but that the fair object of your adoration is as fully sensible of your devotion to her as you are yourself. Do you think she does not see through your stealthy, hastily-averted glances, your nervous hand-pressures, your laboriously easy and graceful attitudes? Women have in these matters of the heart an instinct which *never lies.* Sooner or later your secret will be discovered, and no ostrich flying to bury her head in the desert sand will be more defenceless, more utterly powerless to conceal itself than you.

When Launcelot Trevor took leave that night with such an approving conscience and comfortable sense of a perilous duty well and wisely performed, he little dreamed of the mischief he had wrought, never to be undone till the day when all mistakes shall be rectified. He little dreamed of the long hours that Ida lay awake that night with flushed cheeks and tossed fair hair floating on the pillow, her blue eyes sparkling with the feverish excitement caused by the gratification of a long-cherished and secret desire.

Do not think too harshly of her, my reader ; do not blame her more than she deserves. At this period of her life she was like a spoilt child, well nigh satiated with excitement and adulation, spurning the many wholesome and innocent pleasures around her, and longing, with a child's feverish wilfulness, for the one treasure which had been hitherto out of her reach. She had cried for the moon in the admiration of Lord Trevor, and now that it had fallen at her feet (following the analogy of the spoilt child), she scarcely knew whether to be most surprised or alarmed, yet she could not help feeling gratified at the admiration (suppressed and covert as it was) of such a man as Lord Trevor. The triumph, such as it was, was innocent

enough on her part; she dreamed of
no disloyalty to Arthur; nay, she even
thought, with amused pride, of his surprise when she should tell him that his
flinty-hearted friend had at last been compelled to do homage to her charms. Lord
Trevor's tardy attentions flattered and
pleased her; to the possibility of his *love*
she never cast a thought.

END OF VOL. I.

BILLING AND SONS, PRINTERS, GUILDFORD, SURREY.

www.ingramcontent.com/pod-product-compliance
Lightning Source LLC
Chambersburg PA
CBHW030619030726
47497CB00006B/1556